DAVID
COPPERFIELD

Retold by Christine Cotting

Contents

CHAPTER

PAGE

1   I Am Born   2

2   My World and Its Changes   8

3   My Year at Boarding School   32

4   My First Life in London   54

5   On the Road to the Future   74

6   Somebody Turns Up   98

7   Out of School and Into the World   106

8   New Love and Old Friends   142

9   Losses and a Search   154

10   Blissful   164

11 Wickfield and Heep 182

12 My Dora, Again 190

13 Word and Hope 200

14 Money Found, People Lost 216

15 Many Go and One Returns 236

I Am Born

I was born on a Friday, at midnight. The clock began to strike its twelve tones and I gave my first good cry all at the same moment. According to the custom of those superstitious times, the hour and day of my birth were thought to set me up for an unlucky life, and for the dubious privilege of seeing ghosts and spirits. I was born at Blunderstone, in the eastern England county of Suffolk. The house where I was born was called "The Rookery" for the crows my father mistakenly believed lived in the surrounding trees. In fact, on the night of my birth, both crows and father were no longer there, the crows gone who-knows-where, and father moved to a graveplot in the neighboring churchyard.

Some ten hours before my birth, on a bright, windy March afternoon, my mother sat by the fire, feeling sick and sad, mourning the loss of her much-older husband and my impending arrival. Her eye was caught by a strange woman coming through the garden toward the house. Tall and rigid and stern-looking, the woman stepped directly to the parlor window, pressing the end of her nose hard against the glass.

My mother took such a fright at the odd woman's popping up in the window not three feet away that she fled behind a chair in the far corner.

The stranger looked from one side of the room to the other, examining it fully from her window perch, and motioned to my mother to open the door.

"Mrs. David Copperfield, I think," said the visitor, giving Mother a long look.

"Yes," my mother said faintly.

"I'm Miss Betsey Trotwood, your late husband's aunt. I trust you've heard of me," was the brisk introduction, and Miss Betsey stepped past my mother into the hallway.

Heard of her indeed! This aunt was well-known in the family, and well thought to be unusual and difficult, and all my mother had ever heard disturbed her so much that she grew faint, breaking down into sobs. This dreadful visitor on top of all the rest that she was going through was too much to take.

"When do you expect—" Miss Betsey began when Mother's crying had stopped.

"I'm so frightened," said my mother. "I don't know what's wrong. I'm sure I'm going to die from all of this."

"No, no! It's nothing to worry about. Let's have some tea, and it will settle you down." Miss Betsey called for Peggotty, the housekeeper, to bring tea, and seated herself by the fire.

"I have no doubt your child will be a girl, my dear," she assured my mother. "It *must* be a girl. And from the moment of this girl's birth, I intend to be her friend, her godmother, and I want you to call her Betsey Trotwood Copperfield. She must be well brought up—I'll make that my work."

The look of my mother when Peggotty

delivered the hot tea prompted an immediate call for the doctor, and mother was taken to her room to lie down.

Dr. Chillip arrived and passed the hours until midnight either attending to Mother or sitting by the hearth with the strange and sturdy woman whose bonnet was tied neatly over her left arm, and whose ears were stuffed to overflowing with wads of cotton placed against any unpleasant sounds that might slip down the steps.

At half-past midnight, the doctor brought happy news to Miss Betsey that I had arrived, a fine and healthy boy. Without a word, she rose, took her bonnet by the strings, and aimed a blow at Dr. Chillip's head. She clamped the bonnet, bent and silly-looking, back on her head, walked out the door, and never looked back.

It would be some years before we really met.

CHAPTER 2

My World
and Its Changes

My mother was beautiful, with silky, long hair and a youthful shape. Peggotty, with no shape at all and eyes so black they seemed to darken her whole face, had such red and firm cheeks and arms that I expected birds to peck at her instead of the apples that lay in the orchard. One of my earliest memories is of the touch of Peggotty's forefinger, roughened by sewing to feel like a cheese grater, held out for my balance as I tottered back and forth between the two of them.

Our house was two-storied, with the kitchen on the ground floor. There were two main rooms—parlors we called them then—one where Mother and Peggotty and I sat each evening, for we were all a family, and one where we sat less comfortably on Sundays and holidays.

On the night when everything began to change, Peggotty and I sat in the parlor, she sewing and I reading to her about the habits of crocodiles.

The garden bell rang, and we went out the door. My mother, looking unusually pretty, stood speaking to a man with the blackest, shiniest hair and beard—the same man who had walked her home from church on Sunday.

Mother picked me up and the man patted my head, but somehow I didn't like him or his deep voice, or the way his hand touched my mother's hand in touching me, and I pushed away from him.

Later, I was wakened from a half-sleep in the parlor by Mother and Peggotty arguing.

"Not someone like him! Mr. Copperfield wouldn't have liked that," said Peggotty.

"You'll drive me crazy!" my mother cried. "I don't care what other people are saying. Nothing is settled between the two of us. And how can you accuse me of not caring for Davy?

"Am I a bad mother to you, Davy?" she asked, coming to the chair where I lay and putting her cheek against mine. Although I wasn't certain what caused our tears, we all began crying together, a great flood that lasted all night if the sniffles and quiet sobs that filled our darkened house were any proof.

In the next weeks and months, the black-whiskered man came by after church and at other times. And the more often he appeared, the less Peggotty seemed to spend her evenings with us in the parlor. I came to know him as "Mr. Murdstone," and I liked him no better than at first, having an uneasy jealousy of him in the way he drew my mother's attention.

One evening when Mother was out, Peggotty and I sat in the parlor, with sewing thread and crocodiles to entertain us.

"Davy, how would you like to go along with me to spend a couple of weeks at my brother's place by the sea?" Peggotty asked. "There are boats and ships, and fishermen, and the beach."

"It would be wonderful, Peggotty, but what would Mother say? And what will she do while we're away? She can't stay by herself," I said.

"She'll let us go," Peggotty assured me.

And she did, calling it a wonderful plan. We were to go in a horse-drawn cart after breakfast, and I was almost too excited to sleep.

It touches me now to think how eager I was to leave my happy home that morning—and to think how I never guessed I was leaving that happiness forever.

We were headed to Yarmouth behind the slowest horse in the world. The driver himself mimicked his horse, sitting with his elbows on his knees and his head drooping sleepily forward, his greatest activity a breathy and constant whistle.

Peggotty carried a basket of sandwiches and fruits, and we ate and napped the hours away. She always went to sleep with her chin on the handle of the basket, never letting her grip on it relax, and I was amazed how loudly one woman could snore sitting up.

The flatness and the smells of Yarmouth! Town and tide seemed to blend so completely it was hard to tell the land from the sea, even in their colors. The streets smelled of fish and tar, and they bustled with sailors on foot and in carts. We walked on solid roads strewn with woodchips and sand, past boatbuilders' yards, riggers' lofts, and blacksmiths' forges, until we reached the liquid stretch of the town.

"There's the house, Davy." Peggotty directed my gaze with a nod of her bonnet toward the sea.

I looked in all directions, as far as I could stare, but all I saw was a black barge or some other kind of very old boat, not far off, high and dry on the ground, with an iron funnel sticking out of it for a chimney and smoking very cozily. I certainly saw nothing that would pass for a house in my experience.

"That ship-looking thing?" I asked.

"That's it," she said and led me toward it, and aboard.

There was a door cut in the side, and it was roofed in, and there were little windows all around, but the wonderful charm of it was that it was a real boat that had surely been upon the water hundreds of times. All inside was beautifully clean and tidy, and my room in the stern was whitewashed and so sunny the patchwork bedspread made my eyes ache with its brightness. Peggotty's brother, Daniel, dealt in lobster and crabs and crawfish, and their smell was everywhere, even more pervasive than the sunshine.

Daniel, cherry-cheeked like his sister, was a large and friendly man—"good as gold and true as steel" was Peggotty's description. He welcomed us cheerfully and offered us all that his house contained. Two others lived there with him, Ham and Em'ly, the children of relatives who had died at sea. Ham, his cousin's son, was huge and strong, a six-foot-tall boy with curly blond hair. Em'ly, his sister's child, was small, shy, and beautiful—and I was immediately certain I was in love.

We spent the days out on the beach picking up stones and shells, Em'ly and I, telling the stories of our young lives and sharing our dreams about the future. Most of all she wanted to live an educated and cultured life in a great city like London or Paris. She feared the sea because of what she had seen it do to boats and people, and was terribly frightened of the storms that rose on the water and tossed even the largest craft around like pieces of a puzzle.

The vacation passed too quickly. I knew that I would miss Daniel and Ham, and the sounds and smells of Yarmouth, but most I dreaded leaving Em'ly. We promised to write, and we did for a while thereafter. Our futures were destined to be loosely tied to one another for some years— but never in the same carefree and sunny way as those two weeks spent seaside.

The matched set of carthorse and driver came to take us back to Blunderstone Rookery, and as much as I mourned the passing of my time at the shore, I looked forward to returning home to my own nest and to the comfort and

company of my mother. Peggotty, on the other hand, seemed worried and nervous.

It was gloomy when we pulled up outside the Rookery. And when the door opened, it was not my mother but a woman I didn't know at all—a cook, from her appearance.

"Peggotty, where's Mother? Shouldn't she be at home?" I cried.

"Yes, yes, Davy. I'm sure she's here. But wait a moment, and I'll tell you something." Peggotty took me by the hand and led me into the kitchen. She shut the door.

"What's the matter?" I said, frightened and certain that something awful had happened to my mother. "Why hasn't Mama come out to the gate and why have we come in here?"

"I should have told you before, child, but I couldn't find a way to do it," Peggotty said.

"Tell me now, Peggotty. Tell me now."

"Davy, you've got a father!"

I trembled and turned white. Something— I don't know what—connected with the grave in the churchyard next door and the raising of the dead, seemed to strike me like an unhealthy wind.

"A new one, I mean," said Peggotty.

"A new one?" I repeated.

"Come and see him and—"

"I don't want to see him. I don't want a father!" I backed away toward the kitchen table.

"Then come and see your mother, Davy. You want to see your mother, don't you?" Peggotty asked, holding out her hand and nodding at me.

She led me to the Sunday parlor and left me there. On one side of the fire sat my mother; on the other, Mr. Murdstone of the night-black beard and hair. My mother dropped her embroidery and rose hurriedly but, I thought, timidly.

"Control yourself, Clara, always control yourself," said Mr. Murdstone. "Davy, my boy, how do you do?" He put out a cold hand and I took it for a short shake; then I turned to my mother.

She kissed me and patted my shoulder, but said nothing and seemed unable to meet my gaze. For my part, I couldn't look at her either, or at him. We stood silently and awkwardly for a few moments until they both sat down, and I went to the window to stare out at some shrubs that drooped in the cold.

After a time I left the room and went up-stairs. My old bedroom was moved—at least the things in it—to a room farther down the

hall from my mother's room. Nothing about my house was the same.

But these were just the first of the changes.

I went alone to my room and sat with my small hands crossed over my knees, staring at the wall. I felt cold and dejected, missing the seashore and Em'ly and Daniel, missing the robust activity of Yarmouth, missing the feeling of being a wanted member of a family—missing my life as I had known it to this minute. And when the weight of this unhappiness became too much, I wrapped up in the bedspread and fell asleep in as tight a knot as I could make of myself.

The tug of covers being taken from my head awakened me. Peggotty and Mother had come to look for me, and it was one of them who unwrapped me.

"Davy," said my mother, "what's wrong? Why are you up here like this away from everyone?"

I turned over on my stomach to hide the way my lips were trembling. "Nothing's wrong," I whispered. And I began to cry in earnest, shaking and sobbing at the furthest edge of my bed, away from Mother and Peggotty.

"Davy, you naughty boy!" cried my mother angrily. "When I should most expect to have some happiness, so soon after my new marriage, you behave like this. Oh, dear me!"

I felt the touch of a hand that I knew was neither hers nor Peggotty's, and I slipped to my feet at the far side of the bed. Mr. Murdstone kept his hand on my arm and tightened his grip.

"What's this, Clara, my dear? Have you forgotten? Be firm!" he said in his low and rumbling voice.

"I am very sorry, Edward," said my mother, turning away from all of us and looking instead at the carpet.

"Go downstairs, Clara. You go, too, Peggotty. David and I will be down shortly," said Mr. Murdstone.

The women left the room, Peggotty giving me several worried glances. When we two were left alone, he shut the door and sat on a chair, standing me before him. We looked steadily into one another's eyes, and I seemed to hear my heart beat fast and hard.

"David," he said, making his lips thin by pressing them together, "if I have a difficult horse to deal with, what do you think I do?"

"I don't know."

"I beat him."

I had answered in a sort of breathless whisper, but I felt in the silence after his cold words that my breath grew even shorter.

"I make him hurt. I say to myself, 'I'll conquer that fellow,' and if it costs him all the life he has, I do it." He looked hard at me for several minutes. "You're an intelligent boy, and I know you understand what I am saying to you. Now wash your face and come downstairs with me."

We ate supper alone, the three of us—Peggotty no longer welcome at the table. I gathered from what was said that Mr. Murdstone's sister was coming to stay with us, arriving later that evening. And when the sound of a coach approaching the gate drew us all to the yard shortly after dessert, I followed my mother out the door. She put her hand behind her and held mine as we walked through the garden, until we came close to where Mr. Murdstone stood. Then she took her hand from me and slipped her arm through his.

It was a sour-looking woman who emerged from the carriage. She was dark like her brother, with bushy black eyebrows and a large nose. They were clearly related. She brought with her two rigid black boxes, with her initials on the lids in hard brass nails. When she paid the coachman she took her coins from a small steel purse, and she kept the purse in a jail of a bag that hung from her arm by a heavy chain and shut like a bite. I had never seen such a metallic woman as this Miss Murdstone, and I stared in dread.

The very next morning, long before day-light, Miss Murdstone was up and ringing her bell to wake the household. When Mother came down to prepare tea for breakfast, our houseguest shooed her aside. "Now, Clara, my dear. I am here to relieve you of all the trouble I can. You're much too pretty and thoughtless to have any duties that I can't undertake. Just give me your keys and I'll take care of everything from now on."

From that moment, my mother was a furnishing in her own house. Miss Murdstone kept the keys on her belt or under her pillow at all times. And at those rare moments when the loss of all authority disturbed my mother enough to make her cry in frustration, her husband counseled her to control herself and be firm.

Firmness seemed the grand quality on which both Mr. Murdstone and his sister took their stand. But in fact it was only another name for tyranny and for a certain gloomy and arrogant evil in both of them.

There began to be talk of my going to boarding school. The Murdstones proposed the idea and my mother, of course, agreed, but nothing was done about it. For about six months, I took my lessons at home. These were conducted by my mother, but Mr. Murdstone and his sister were always present and their presence was always felt.

During that time I saw no other children of my age because the Murdstones believed all children to be small vipers. And each day I felt more and more shut out and alienated from my mother. I grew more lonely every day.

All that gave me any comfort was a small collection of my father's books in an upstairs room. Robinson Crusoe, Don Quixote, the Vicar of Wakefield kept alive my imagination and my hope of something beyond that sad existence. Reading was my only pleasure, and when I recall that time the picture always comes to mind of a summer evening, with the sound of boys at play in the churchyard next door, and I sitting on my bed, reading as if my life depended on it.

On what was to be the last day of my lessons at home—and an unusually unhappy day—I found Mr. Murdstone making a whip out of strips of cane when I entered the parlor. My mother and Miss Murdstone sat waiting.

"Now, David, you must be far more careful in your studies today than usual," he said as he slapped the cane across his palm and took a seat.

I was so frightened by the threat that the lessons went badly. At last, even my mother broke under the tension in the room and began to cry.

"David, your stupidity is too much for your poor mother," the man said. "Go upstairs, boy."

He walked me to my room slowly and gravely—I am certain he was delighted by that formal parade toward the execution of justice —and when we got there he suddenly twisted my head beneath his arm.

"Mr. Murdstone! Please don't beat me," I cried. "I have tried to learn, but I can't while you're so close by. I can't!"

"Can't? Or *won't*, boy?" he said.

He had my head in a vice-grip, but I pulled around somehow and stopped him for a moment, once again pleading with him not to beat me. It slowed him little, and I felt the cane crack against me heavily an instant later, and in that same instant I caught his hand in my teeth and bit down into it. He beat me terribly then, as if he would beat me to death. Over the noise of the cane and his grunts and my sobs, I heard running on the stairs. Mother and Peggotty were crying out to stop the torture. Then he was gone, and the door to the room was locked from the outside.

29

I lay on the floor, hurting and furious, listening to the sudden unnatural silence. Hours passed. It grew dark. I was sitting at the window when Miss Murdstone brought me supper, saying not a word and locking the door on her way out. No one else came to see about me.

I remember waking the next morning, feeling cheerful and fresh for the first moment and then being weighed down by the memory of where I was and what had happened the day before. Miss Murdstone and the food she brought me were the only contacts I had with the rest of the house, until the fifth night when I heard Peggotty's whisper at the keyhole.

"Be as quiet as a mouse, Davy," Peggotty warned me when I answered her call, and I knew she meant Miss Murdstone might appear at any moment from her room close down the hall.

"How's Mama, Peggotty? Is she very angry with me for biting Mr. Murdstone?" I asked.

"No, dear. But you are going away. To school. Tomorrow. Near London." I could hear her crying softly on the outside of my jail door.

"Won't I see Mama again?"

"Yes, in the morning. Davy, I just came to say that you must never forget me and I'll never forget you. And I'll take care of your mother and never leave her."

"I won't forget, Peggotty."

In the morning, my bags were by the door when I was brought downstairs to the parlor. My mother was red-eyed and pale as she explained that I was going to school for my own good, and that I could come home for the holidays.

Then I was taken through the door to the sluggish horse and driver that had taken me once to Yarmouth, placed aboard, and sent away.

CHAPTER 3

My Year at Boarding School

We hadn't gone half a mile, and my handkerchief was wet through with tears, when Peggotty burst through a hedgerow and flagged the driver to stop. She climbed into the cart with me and squeezed me in her big, warm arms. Without a word she pulled from her pockets some paper bags of cookies and a change purse. These she crammed into the pockets of my jacket, gave me another powerful hug, and hopped down from the cart, signalling the driver to move on.

I watched the spot in the hedge where she disappeared until I could no longer see spot or hedge, then turned around and pulled the purse from my pocket. It was of stiff leather, with a snap, and inside were three bright coins, three shillings in all. There was also a small piece of paper folded over two half-crowns on which my mother had written, "For Davy. With my love."

The driver took me to a public eating house where Mr. Murdstone had sent money ahead for my dinner.

After dinner, it was time to board a coach for London. The ride was long, overnight and into the next day. My fellow passengers slept soundly and snored most of the night, but I don't recall as much as napping.

When we got to the coach stop in London, there was no one to claim me. I went into the station and passed some time behind the counter with the clerk. My mind was in a flight. Suppose nobody ever came for me. Could I sleep at night in one of the wooden bins with the luggage, and wash at the pump in the horseyard? Was this the final part of Mr.

Murdstone's elaborate plan to get rid of me? If I started off at once and tried to find my way back home, how far could I get before I was hopelessly lost? Could I join the Navy or the Army? Would they take such a little fellow? All of this had my mind in a fever when a man, unhealthy looking and poorly dressed, entered and whispered to the clerk, who lifted me off the baggage scales where I sat and handed me across the counter.

"You're the new boy, I suppose," he said quietly to me. "I'm a teacher at Salem House."

He took me to a school enclosed by a high brick wall. A stout man with a bull-neck, a wooden leg, sagging jowls, and a close-cut cap of hair answered the door. We entered the courtyard in front of a square brick building with two wings and a bare and unfurnished appearance. It was perfectly silent. When I asked about this, I was told everyone was away on holiday and I was here early to begin my studies as a punishment.

In the forlorn and desolate classroom, papers and dirt covered the floor and desks; mice ran everywhere looking for food. My teacher, Mr. Mell, took me to the back of the room, where I spied a cardboard sign, beautifully written, that bore the warning, "Beware of him. He bites."

"Where's the dog?" I asked Mr. Mell.

"What dog?"

"Isn't there a dog to wear this sign, sir?" I pointed to the cardboard.

"No, Copperfield," Mr. Mell said gravely. "I'm afraid that's not a dog, but a boy. My instructions are to put this sign around your neck and hang it down your back. I'm sorry to do it, but I must."

What I suffered from that sign nobody can imagine. I always thought someone was reading it and laughing at me or judging me to be hopeless. And in the weeks before the school filled up again with students, I lived in dread of their return and my humiliation. In later years as I recalled Salem House, I could see the dirty bricks, the green cracked flagstones in the courtyard, the discolored trunks of some of the grim and dying trees. I could smell and feel the damp of the rooms. But more acutely than anything else, I remembered the sign and how I hated it.

I had been at my studies about a month when the school's headmaster, Mr. Creakle, and all the other boys returned from their holidays.

On the evening of Mr. Creakle's return, I was taken by Mr. Tungay, the man with the wooden leg, to meet the headmaster. Mr. Creakle had a snug garden space that looked like an oasis after the miniature-desert of a playground I had grown used to. I trembled as I followed the uneven clomp of Tungay's leg down the passageway, and was led before a stout man with a fiery face and little pig-eyes. There were thick veins in his forehead, above a small nose and a huge chin. He was bald on top, but some thin and wet-looking strands of greying hair were combed up and forward to meet just above his brows. What made the greatest impression on me was his voice—he had none, but spoke in a strained whisper that required such exertion as to make his angry face even more furious and his ropy veins even more bulging.

"So, this is the biter, is it?" said Mr. Creakle when I took a place before his chair. "What's the report on him?"

"Nothing against him yet, sir," was the wooden-legged man's response. "There's been no chance for mischief."

I thought Mr. Creakle looked disappointed by this news.

"I have the happiness of knowing your stepfather, Mr. Murdstone," whispered Mr. Creakle, taking me by the ear with a nasty twist. "What a fine man of strong character!"

My ear took another painful pinch.

"Let me tell you something about myself," he whispered menacingly. "When I say I'll do a thing, I do it. And when I say I'll have a thing done, I will have it done. Nothing gets in my way. Do you get that, boy? Now you begin to know me like the other boys do. Take him away."

The first boy to come back, Tommy Traddles, appeared the next morning. He took real delight in my awful sign and saved me the embarrassment of either displaying or hiding it by presenting me to every other boy and getting the fun-making out of the way. Some of the boys couldn't resist the temptation to pretend I was a dog and instructed me to roll over or sit up, but none of it was mean-spirited.

By the end of the day, I had met all the boys but one, James Steerforth, widely reputed to be the central figure among all the students. He was said to be a great scholar, extremely handsome, and at least half a dozen years older than I. When we met that night he pronounced my punishment a terrible shame—and became an instant friend.

Mr. Creakle's reputation for violence certainly was not exaggerated. On the first day of classes, the roar of voices in the classroom was suddenly silenced when Mr. Creakle appeared in the doorway after breakfast. Mr. Tungay waited to his left as his interpreter, ready to repeat in a shout what his master said in a whisper.

"Be silent!" shouted Tungay, although there was not a sound in the room. "Boys, this is a new semester," he repeated for Mr. Creakle. "Come prepared to learn, I advise you, because I come prepared to punish you. Now get to work!"

Creakle began his passage up and down the aisles of boys bent over their notebooks. He came to where I sat and told me that if I were famous for biting, he was famous for biting, too.

"What do you think of the teeth on this?" he asked, putting his fiery-faced whistle near my

ear and snapping his cane whip across my legs.
"Sharp, hey? A double set of teeth, hey? Has a
deep bite, doesn't it?" With every question, he
let the cane cut into my back or my arms.

He greeted the majority of the boys in the
room in a similar manner, doing so with enor-
mous delight. Eventually nearly every child present was crying or cowering in his seat.

In such an atmosphere, how, then, did I
manage to pick up some crumbs of knowledge? It was because of the friends I had at
Salem House, especially Tommy Traddles and
James Steerforth. Tommy's companionship in
the face of our mutual adversity, and Steerforth's steady championing of the interests of
the younger and weaker boys went a long way
toward protecting my spirit and some small
way toward protecting my skin.

Steerforth was not usually punished like
the rest of the boys. He was older and larger,
and his attitude suggested he was not much
impressed by Creakle's cane. In fact, Creakle

and the teachers, even the brute with the wooden leg, generally left Steerforth alone. He was my protector and friend, although his protection did not keep me from regular beatings in and out of class.

And if it can be agreed that something good comes from even the most evil thing, in his severity Mr. Creakle found the sign hanging down my back to be in his way when he hit me with the whip, so he ordered it removed for good.

In this fearful and tormented way, the semester passed. Most of the time is a jumble in my recollection: the ending of summer and the changing of the seasons; the frosty mornings when we were bell-clanged out of bed before dawn; the cold, cold smell of the dark nights when we huddled under light and scratchy blankets; the morning schoolroom, which was nothing but a great shivering-machine; the daily choice of tasteless beef, boiled or roasted, and clods of bread-and-butter; the dog-eared books, cracked slates, tear-stained notebooks; beatings with cane whips or rulers; and the grimy atmosphere of ink surrounding all.

At last, the holidays arrived! How strange it felt to be going home when it was not home, and to find that every object I packed reminded me of the happy old times—all like a dream that I could never dream again! I wondered as

I traveled if it might not have been better to stay at school and remember things as I wished them to be. But soon I was at our house, where the bare old elm trees wrung their many hands in the bleak winter air and shreds of the old crows' nests drifted away on the wind.

I jumped down from the coach at the garden gate and took the path toward the house, glancing at the windows and fearing to see Mr. Murdstone or his metallic sister staring out at me. I opened the door silently and a sweet memory of my earliest years greeted me: my mother was humming a lullaby she had sung to me so long ago, her soft voice sweet and clear.

She was sitting by the fire as I took a timid step into the parlor.

"Mother," I said quietly, and she came quickly across to me.

"Davy, my dear, dear boy! You're home at last," she said, hugging me long and close.

Peggotty, hearing our voices, came bounding in from the kitchen and we all plopped down on the carpet and laughed and hugged and cried.

Mr. Murdstone and his sister were out on a visit and were not likely to return before night, so we could spend our afternoon together as we had before our threesome was increased to five. We ate supper by the fireside. Peggotty brought out my old dinner plate with the large ship and stormy waters painted in the center, and the mug with my name on it, and my little fork and the knife that wouldn't cut.

We talked of neighbors and I shared the few happy stories of my life at Salem House, telling all about Tommy and Steerforth and never mentioning Mr. Creakle or Mr. Tungay. I noticed that my mother, though she smiled a lot, seemed more serious and careworn. She was still pretty, but looked too delicate, so pale and thin she seemed transparent. Her hands trembled a bit and she was nervous.

After the dishes were cleared away, I moved close to Mother's side and sat with my arms around her waist. It was a wonderful evening. I sat looking at the fire and seeing pictures in the red-hot coals, almost believing that I had never been away, that the Murdstones were only such pictures that would vanish when the fire got low, and that there was nothing real in all that I remembered except my mother, Peggotty, and I.

It was almost ten o'clock when we heard the sound of wheels by the gate. Mother hurried me to bed, and I gladly took a candle and went. It seemed to me, as I walked to the bedroom where I had been imprisoned, that the Murdstones' arrival brought into the house a cold blast of air that blew away the old, familiar feelings like a feather in a gale.

I dreaded going down to breakfast the next morning, and in fact made several starts for the stairs only to run on tiptoe back to the shelter of my room. Mr. Murdstone was standing by the fire in the parlor and Miss Murdstone was pouring tea when I finally went in.

47

He looked at me steadily, but made no sign of recognition.

After a moment of confusion, I went toward him and said, "I beg your pardon, sir. I am very

sorry for what I did and I hope you will forgive me."

"I'm glad to hear you're sorry, David," he said, putting the once-bitten hand out for a brief shake, then turning away from me entirely.

"Dear me," sighed Miss Murdstone. "How long are the holidays?"

"A month, ma'am," I said.

"Counting from when?"

"From today, ma'am."

"Oh," she puffed. "Then there's *one* day off."

Each morning she took her calendar and checked off a day. She did it gloomily until she came to ten, and then became more hopeful. As the page filled with Xs, she turned almost pleasant.

The holidays slogged by until the morning came when Miss Murdstone made her last X and said, "Here's the last day off!"

I wasn't sorry to go, for I was looking forward to Steerforth and Tommy. I kissed Peggotty and my mother, and knew that I would miss them, but there was a gulf between us and the parting had been there every day of my vacation. I took with me the memories that would best keep me and left behind those that hurt.

I had been back at Salem House two months when my tenth birthday dawned. The morning class had only begun when one of the schoolmasters sent me to the parlor. It must be a box of birthday cookies and treats from Peggotty, I thought as I hurried down the hallway. Something to brighten the day for me and the other boys, for anyone lucky enough to receive packages shared any food received with every other boy.

I skidded around the open parlor door, practically knocking Mrs. Creakle to the floor. She held an opened letter in her hand, but there was no box of treats in sight.

"David Copperfield," she said, leading me to a sofa and sitting down beside me, "I have something to tell you, child."

She glanced at the letter on her lap and took my hand in hers. "It's a bad lesson, but we all have to learn it some time, some of us when we're young. Was your mother ill when you were home for vacation?" she asked.

I felt a chill even colder than the day. "No, ma'am," I whispered, the tears beginning to run from my eyes before I knew how bad the news would be.

"She's dead," was all I heard Mrs. Creakle say, although it seemed her mouth kept moving as I stared through the blur of tears.

Mrs. Creakle kept me with her all day, sometimes sitting and holding me while I cried, sometimes leaving me alone with my thoughts and my sadness. I thought of our house closed up and hushed, and for the first time I felt truly an orphan in the world.

The next afternoon I left Salem House, traveling by coach to Yarmouth and then on to Suffolk. The long and unhappy trip ended at the garden gate, and I was in Peggotty's strong arms before I got close to the kitchen door. We cried for some time, kneeling on the stone walkway, then finally she scooped me up and bundled me inside, all the time talking in whispers to calm herself and me.

I sat for a while in the parlor where the only sound was the hiss and crackle of logs on the

fire. Mr. Murdstone sometimes would walk from chair to table to sofa and then to chair again. He seemed to be the only restless thing, except the clocks, in the whole motionless house.

On the third day, we gathered around an open space in the neighboring churchyard, beside my father's gravestone, and heard prayers spoken over the only family I had. Soon it was finished and we walked back to the garden gate and into the kitchen.

"She wasn't well for a long time, Davy," said Peggotty. "And she wasn't happy. She seemed to get weaker every day. But, Davy, the last time I saw her acting anything like her old self was the night you came home for vacation. She loved you, don't you ever forget."

I sat that evening in the parlor, alone with my earliest recollections of my mother, thinking of her winding her curls round and round her index finger, and dancing and laughing with me at twilight in that very room.

CHAPTER 4

My First
Life in London

The day after my mother's funeral, Peggotty was fired from Blunderstone Rookery. With the unhappy changes that had come into the place, I hardly think she minded leaving, but she worried terribly about me and how I would manage in such a grey and uncaring environment.

I wondered, too, what was next for me. When would I return to school? Or would one of the Murdstones be taking on the chore of my education? When at last I mustered the courage to ask Miss Murdstone about Salem House, she said she thought I would not be returning. No one seemed very interested in me.

Peggotty decided to go to Yarmouth and stay with her brother until she could find work. The Murdstones' dislike of me was evident and she thought they might well agree to let me travel with her for a stay by the sea. To be surrounded again by the honest and smiling faces of Daniel, Ham, and, best of all, Em'ly; to spend Sunday mornings listening to the bells ringing and watching shadowy ships breaking through the mist; to search the beach for shells and pebbles—such a wonderful way to live!

Peggotty had little difficulty getting permission for my going with her.

"The boy will be lazy and useless there," Miss Murdstone declared, "and idleness is the beginning of every evil. But he'd be idle here, too—or anywhere, I'd say. So to save my brother the annoyance of looking after him, he can go."

And so we did. Mr. Barkis, the cartdriver who carried all travelers from Blunderstone to Yarmouth and who had taken me several times on my trips to and from Salem House, came to get us. Barkis was a bachelor, cheerful and gentle enough. He took real notice of Peggotty and his attentions made her blush and laugh like a young girl. By the time we arrived in Yarmouth, the two of them had decided to see one another again when Barkis made his next trip to the waterside village.

The Peggotty cottage looked just the way I remembered, but a bit smaller. My room was exactly as it had been, clean and sparkling in the sunshine coming through the porthole.

After dinner that evening we sat by the fire, Peggotty knitting and rocking, Daniel and Ham sucking on pipes full of apple-sweet tobacco, Em'ly staring at the dancing flames, and the conversation turned to my not returning to Salem House. Saying I would miss my friends Traddles and Steerforth, I launched into a long and glowing description of their many virtues. I was well into the talk of Steerforth's good character, good grades, and good looks before I noticed the attention Em'ly was paying to my words.

"He's as brave as a lion," I said, "and smart and funny. Such a speaker that he can win anybody to his side, and he sings, too."

I was unknowingly sealing Em'ly's fate. The romantic picture I painted of the marvelous Steerforth was enough to enchant any young girl.

The time spent in Yarmouth flew past. I'd never seen such sky and water and marvelous ships as when I sat in the doorway of the creaky old boat, letting my eyes fill with memories to carry back to the gloom of Blunderstone.

Barkis visited many times during those weeks. He was friendly to everyone, but he had only one interest: Peggotty. Barkis was not a man used to courting women, but he was clearly fascinated with Peggotty. He never came without a gift—a bundle of oranges tied in a napkin, a pair of ebony earrings, a huge pincushion, some Spanish onions, two boxes of dominoes, a canary in a cage, a leg of pickled pork. Peggotty was enchanted, and before the weeks of my stay in Yarmouth were over, she and Barkis were married.

On the trip back home, Peggotty made sure I knew she would never abandon me to the neglect of the Murdstones. "You'll always have a home with Barkis and me, Davy," she said again and again. "If you go as far as China, you can always come home to me."

Life in The Rookery was a sort of solitary confinement. I had no companions other than my own thoughts and my father's books. The harsh and grimy ruin of Salem House would have been more pleasant than the loneliness I felt at home. I wasn't beaten or starved, not actively mistreated. Just disliked and overlooked, and made to feel like a wrinkle in the Murdstones' otherwise comfortable clothing. Month after month, I was simply neglected. When they were at home, I had my meals with them in silence; when they were away, I was alone, caring for myself. It was well into late autumn when Mr. Murdstone announced an abrupt change in the course of my life.

"David, this is Mr. Quinion, a manager at Murdstone and Grinby in London," he said, introducing me to a dinner guest one evening. "He has inquired about your education and I've told him you're no longer in school—that you aren't doing much but lying around reading or staring out the window."

"To the young, this is a world of action, my boy," Mr. Quinion joined in. "Not for moping, not for wasting time!" He smiled at me kindly, but, I thought, with a little greediness in his look.

"I'm not a rich man, David," Mr. Murdstone began again. "Your education thus far has been costly. But I don't think more schooling will do you any good. It's time you stepped out to begin your fight with the world on your own terms." He turned toward the fire and I stole a glance at Miss Murdstone who sat sewing and smiling. "So, you'll go with Mr. Quinion to our warehouse in London and work there. You'll earn enough to provide you with food and spending money. I've paid for a place for you to live and your laundry will be done for you.

"In short," he concluded, "you're going to begin life on your own. And good luck."

Although I knew that this arrangement was made to get rid of me, I was neither pleased nor frightened. Rather, the entire thing came so out of the blue that when I was packed up and sent off with Mr. Quinion the next morning, I was too confused to know how I felt about the future.

I sat in the carriage with all that I owned stashed in a small, black trunk, and watched the garden gate, the church steeple, and the neighboring graveyard slip out of my sight.

The Murdstone and Grinby bottling warehouse was at the water's edge at the end of a narrow street that curved downhill to the river. It was an old building with a boat dock of its own. The paneled rooms, discolored with the dirt and smoke of a hundred years, the rotting floors and stairways, and the squeaking and scuffling of hundreds of grey rats in the cellar were its only features.

There was a corner of the main floor set aside for bottle cleaning and labeling. Here a few men and several boys examined old bottles against the light from the sooty windows. The cracked or broken ones were tossed in a heap, and the others were washed and rinsed.

Into the noise of breaking glass and the hiss of steamy water, I followed Mr. Quinion on the first morning.

"You, boy!" Quinion shouted at a couple of sweaty, dirty youngsters bent over a crate of bottles. "Over here, fast now!"

"What is it you want, captain?" The taller boy straightened and approached us.

"This is a new boy for the work. See that he learns the ropes and keep him busy."

"Mealy, make room for another pair of hands!" said the boy, directing me to the crate. "What d'they call you?"

"Davy," I shouted. "Davy Copperfield."

"I'm Mick and he's Mealy Potatoes—at least that's what everybody calls him," Mick explained.

Mick and Mealy showed me how to sort the bottles and where to wash them. They pointed out the boxes of labels and the bags of corks to be fitted to all the clean ones. And they talked about their lives outside the warehouse, of their fathers who were bargemen living most of the time on the river, and of Mealy's little sister who danced at a theatre uptown. All the while I worked, I thought how different these boys were from those at Salem House, so unlike Traddles and Steerforth. So unlike me. As I sank into this uneasy companionship, I ached for my dreams of learning and of growing into some kind of distinguished and educated manhood. Trapped was what I felt, trapped and smothered in the musty, ratty warehouse.

At day's end, Mr. Quinion returned and took me to the manager's office. A large man sat waiting there. His clothes were shabby and a little too small, and he carried a sort of walking stick with a large pair of rusty tassels hanging from it. There was no more hair on his head than on a hen's egg, his face bulged out over a stiff, tight collar, and a magnifying glass hung from a long cord around his neck.

"David, this is Mr. Micawber," Mr. Quinion said, closing the door behind us.

"Master Copperfield." Micawber bowed his head briskly and tapped the stick's tip for punctuation. "So glad." Tap. "So glad. You're to take a room at my house, and I think you'll be comfortable there. Mrs. Micawber and our babies will make you feel right at home, I'm sure. So glad. So glad." Again the stick tapped. A brisk spin toward Mr. Quinion, and another tap.

"So, we're off then, sir." Tap. "I'll take David to the house so he won't get lost in our great city." Tap. "Good-day. Good-day." Tap. Tap.

The Micawber house was in Windsor Terrace—a neighborhood every bit as shabby as its tenants, but better than the waterfront. I was presented to Mrs. Micawber, a thin and faded woman carrying twin infants on her hips, and to two other toddlers, a girl and a boy. My room, at the housetop, was scarcely furnished.

While I stayed with them, the only visitors I ever saw or heard of were people to whom Mr. Micawber owed money ... and they were many. They would come by at all hours, day and night, and some were fierce. One dirty-faced man, a bootmaker, would stand on the front porch as early as seven a.m. and shout through the door at Mr. Micawber.

"Come out here!" the bootmaker would yell. "You're in there, I know you are. Pay me what you owe me and be rid of me for good!"

When no miraculous cash was thrust out the door or tossed through the window, he upped his verbal attack to include the words "robbers" and "thieves." This was no more effective—not because Micawber was dishonest, not because he had any quarrel with the amounts owed, but because there was barely enough money to put milk on the table. He wasn't a lazy man—in fact, he was busy every day trying to make a go of one effort or another. And he was unfailingly optimistic, absolutely convinced that something wonderful was just around the next corner.

"Something will turn up," he said several times a day. His confidence was amazing in the face of great proof to the contrary, and I tried to imitate his positive attitude in my own bitter surroundings at the warehouse.

Mr. Micawber's money woes eventually came to a crisis. He was arrested early one morning for his debts and taken to the King's Bench Prison to work off some of what he owed.

I took my few things to another boarding-house in the neighborhood and, not yet 12 years old, continued on the business of making my own way in the world.

Several months passed and Mr. Micawber's petition for release from debtors' prison was approved. He was freed as well from his creditors. He moved his family to a small house near mine, but soon decided to move them out of London to a country place near Plymouth. Exactly what he would do there he had no idea. "Something will turn up," he assured me. "It always does, you know."

Micawber made travel plans for the weekend. I'd grown so accustomed to this family and was so truly friendless without them that the idea of being alone again was too awful to be considered. I began to form a radical plan.

On their last night in London, the Micawbers invited me to dinner. Over pork roast and applesauce, we talked about the our coming separation.

"Master Copperfield," said Mrs. Micawber, passing me a second helping of pudding, "you have never been a boarder in our home. You have been a friend."

"Quite so, Mrs.," said Mr. Micawber. "David, at present, and until something turns up, I have nothing but advice to give you. And it's good advice, although I've not had the sense to take it myself! Never wait for tomorrow when you can do something today. Putting things off steals time from you. Don't let it happen!"

After supper, Mr. Micawber walked me to the door and we said farewell on the front steps.

"Happiness to you, Copperfield! If my bad times have taught you any better way to make a life for yourself, then I'm glad I had them." Tap. Tap. He shook my hand, then leaned the stick against the doorframe and gave me a warm hug. The last thing I heard before I closed my door was "David! Something will turn up."

The next day's bottle scrubbing required the usual small amount of my attention, so I was free to plan an escape from my unhappy surroundings. By day's end I knew there were not many more gritty, rat-bitten days left for me at Murdstone and Grinby. I knew I was running away from London into the countryside to find the only relative I had left in the world—my aunt, Miss Betsey Trotwood.

How this desperate idea came to me I have no idea. But once it had arrived, it planted itself so firmly that no amount of doubt or difficulty would dislodge it. All I knew of my aunt came from the old story of my birthnight—a story that I delighted in hearing my mother tell and retell. My aunt walked into and stomped out of that story, a scary and stern form. But I remembered that, for all the strangeness of her actions the night I was born, my mother had said she sensed a gentleness beneath the hardbitten outer layer, and on that sense I built all my hopes for a better future.

I had no idea where to find Miss Betsey Trotwood, so I wrote to Peggotty, casually mentioning that I had heard of a lady much like Miss
Betsey who lived at a place I made up, and I
wondered if it could be the same person.
Peggotty wrote back, enclosing a small amount
of money, and told me my aunt lived somewhere close to Dover. That was enough for me.

On the last day of the workweek, I left a
message with Mr. Quinion and packed my

black trunk for travel. It was too heavy to drag to the coach-office, so I went looking for someone to help me carry it there.

A long-legged young man with a very small horse cart caught my eye. I went up to him and asked if he might like a job moving a box. I told him where I had left it and where I wanted it moved.

"Righto!" he said and was up behind the donkey and off down the street so quick I had trouble keeping up with him.

We brought the box down and put it on the cart. I needed to attach a label to the top of the box with instructions for the agent at the coach-office, and pulled paper and a pencil from my pocket. The paper pulled my money from my pocket as well and my few precious coins rolled under the young man's cart. Swiftly he was into the street, under the cart, and gripping my fortune in his filthy fingers.

"Why, look what I've found here!" he squealed delightedly. "I've found money someone lost. Well, they won't be back for it, I'm sure. They're long gone now, I'm sure. It's my money now, I'm sure!"

"No!" I cried, jumping toward the cart. "That's mine. Please give it to me."

"What? Trying to steal from a poor man who has just been blest with some rare good luck?" he said. "Get away. This is my fortune. I found it!" And with that he gave the horse's reins a quick snap and the cart jolted away—the man, my money, and my trunk all gone in a flash.

I bolted off behind him, running as fast as I could, but I had not enough breath to catch him. Exhausted and defeated, I gave up the chase and let him go with everything I owned.

I rested several moments against a low wall at the end of a bridge, until my breath came back and a rush of tears with it. Then I turned in the direction of the Dover Road and ran, panting and crying, slowing and speeding, but not stopping until I could run no more.

CHAPTER 5

On the Road to the Future

I traveled on foot for days, at last reaching Dover, hungry, thirsty, and worn out. I asked a carriage driver if he could tell me where Miss Betsey lived.

"Trotwood?" he asked. "I know the name. Old lady?"

I said she was.

"Pretty stiff in the back?" he said, straightening himself up tall.

"Yes," I said. "I think it very likely."

"Is gruff, and speaks sharp?" he asked.

My heart sank as I agreed with the probable accuracy of his description.

He gave me directions and wished me luck in the face of surely being run off her property when I arrived.

A couple of twisty paths led me to a very neat little cottage with bay windows curtained in ruffled white cloth, and a small and perfect garden full of flowers in front. I stood across the lane behind a hedge and peered at the house. I saw no one, heard nothing but birdsong and a distant dog's barking. I looked to the windows in the second floor of the house and saw a face—a pleasant gentleman's face—topped with silver hair. He squinted in my direction, and I saw him laugh and turn away.

I heard a squeaky sound of hinges. A lady with a scarf tied over her hair and a pair of gardener's gloves in her hand stepped out of the cottage. She wore a sturdy-looking apron with many pockets and carried a great knife. She came out the door and off the steps exactly as my mother had described Betsey Trotwood's approach through our garden years before, and I knew it had to be my aunt.

Although this was the moment I'd come for, slogging along the Dover Road for six days and sleeping under the sky for six nights, now I couldn't move from behind that hedge. I looked down at myself—shirt and pants stained with sweat, dew, and grass, and torn in places. My hair hadn't been combed or my face washed since I'd left London, and the sun had tanned all my skin a berry-brown.

Miss Betsey Trotwood knelt in the far corner of her garden, yanking at a root and some offending weeds. It was desperation more than confidence that pushed me from the protection of the hedge, across the lane, and into her tidy yard.

"If you please, ma'am," I began.

Her head snapped up in surprise. "What? Go away! Go! No boys here!" she cried, and shook a soily gloved hand in my direction.

"If you please, Aunt Betsey."

"Eh?" she exclaimed.

"I'm your nephew, David Copperfield."

"Oh, Lord!" said my aunt. And she sat flat down in the garden dirt.

"You came to my house in Blunderstone, The Rookery, on the night I was born and saw my mother. She's dead now and my life has become very unhappy." The story rushed out of me. "I ran away and could only think to come here to you. I was robbed when I first set out, and have walked all the way from London."

Here my self-control gave out all at once and I broke into a raging cry, letting go of all the pent-up fear and exhaustion of the week. Aunt Betsey, looking thunderstruck, sat on the ground staring at me. Then she got up in a great flurry and hurried me into the parlor.

"Mercy on us!" was all she said, but she said it several times as she poured me a glass of some sweet juice from a decanter. She seated me sideways on the sofa, with a shawl under my backside and her head kerchief under my feet.

"Mercy, mercy on us! Janet," my aunt called from the parlor door, "go upstairs and ask Mr. Bick to come down here, please."

I lay quietly on the couch while Aunt Betsey stalked back and forth across the parlor, her hands behind her. In a couple of moments, the man I'd seen in the window upstairs poked his

silver head around the door frame and gave a hearty laugh.

"Don't act the fool, Mr. Bick," said my aunt, "because no one has better sense than you when you put your mind to it. And you must put your mind to it now, if never before. This boy is David Copperfield. You've heard me speak of my nephew, David. Well, this is his son. I don't know how or why he isn't a girl instead of a boy, but he's not and that's all there is to it."

"A boy, yes. A boy indeed." Mr. Bick smiled a big grin at me, but snapped a serious frown across it when he caught a glimpse of Aunt Betsey's scowl.

"He's run away! What shall I do with him?"

"Do with him?" said Mr. Bick feebly, scratching his silver head. "Oh! Do with him?"

There was a long pause while my aunt stared at Mr. Bick and Mr. Bick stared at my aunt.

"Why, if I was you," he began. "If I was, I'd—uh—I'd—I'd wash him! Yup, that's it. I'd wash him."

"Janet, Mr. Bick makes the most sense," my aunt exclaimed to her young housekeeper. "Heat the bath."

While preparations were being made in the back of the cottage, I lay still on the couch, looking first at my aunt and then at Mr. Bick. Aunt Betsey was tall and hard-featured, but not ugly. Her hair was grey and wispy, and her eyes sparkled and darted about like bright bird's eyes. Mr. Bick's silver hair topped a very pink face set on a short neck and hunched shoulders. His grey eyes bulged a bit and had a watery look to them. He seemed not to be able to concentrate deeply or for very long on any one thing, and I suspected he was slow-witted and therefore somehow in the care of my aunt and her housekeeper.

At length the bath was ready. I soaked out much of the aching from the trek and returned to something of my regular grime-free skin color. I dried off and dressed in pants and a flannel shirt contributed by Mr.

Bick, and Aunt Betsey wound me up in three woolen shawls. I napped in the parlor until dinner, and soon after dessert I was shown to my bedroom.

The window beside my bed overlooked the sea where this night the moon sparkled brilliantly. After my tiny candle burned out, I sat looking at the moon and the water, hoping to read my fortune in it. But there was only the quiet, the comfort of the cool breeze, and

the promise of wonderful rest on snow-white sheets.

The next morning's breakfast was difficult. Aunt Betsey was deep in her own thoughts for most of it, and when she'd finished a few bites of muffin and some tea, she sat back, folded her arms, and focused a steady stare on me.

"I've written to him," she said at last.

"To—?"

"To your stepfather. To Mr. Murdstone."

"Does he know where I am, Aunt?" I asked, alarmed. "Will I be returned to him?"

"I want to speak with him about that, David," Aunt Betsey answered. "I don't know just what will happen."

We spent the morning sitting together in her parlor, she writing long letters, I reading. Mr. Bick joined us for a short time, saying nothing but looking out the gardenside window and chuckling loudly for no apparent reason. When he had gone, I ventured a question to my aunt.

"Is Mr. Bick—is he at all out of his mind?"

"Not a bit," she said. "If he is anything at all, he is certainly not that. He has been *called* crazy, even by some good people, but Mr. Bick is just different and has a way of viewing the world that is not the same as everyone else's. He makes people uncomfortable because he makes them question their own views."

"How did he come to be here, Aunt?"

"He's a distant relative of mine, of ours. His brother didn't like having him visible when friends came to call and he sent him off to some private hospital. I heard about it and stepped in. Said I wasn't afraid of him and he would be well cared for here. After a bit of argument, I got him and he's been with me ever since. He's the most friendly and gentle creature on earth, and when he focuses his mind on it, he offers wise advice."

My aunt's generosity to Mr. Bick warmed my heart toward her and encouraged me to think that she would likewise intercede on my behalf with Mr. Murdstone. There was something about her, eccentricities and odd moods aside, to be honored and trusted.

A week later we heard from Mr. Murdstone that he and his sister would be coming at once to meet with Aunt Betsey. My worst fears were at fever pitch on the morning they were expected. My aunt was a bit more stern than usual at breakfast, and she rose slowly when Janet came to say they had arrived.

After a few formalities—"hello" and "please take a seat"—the meeting began.

"This ungrateful boy has deserted friends and job," Mr. Murdstone said.

"His appearance," his sister noted sharply, "is perfectly scandalous and disgraceful."

"This boy," Mr. Murdstone began again, "has caused much domestic upset, both during his mother's life and since. He has a rebellious spirit, a violent temper, and a nasty disposition."

"Of all the boys in the world, I believe this to be the very worst!" Miss Murdstone added.

"Mr. Murdstone, what sort of an education do you propose for David?" my aunt asked. "And toward what sort of a future do you plan to steer his dreams? How do you intend to shelter him and raise him and make the very best man of him?"

"I am here to take David back, to dispose of him as I think proper, and to deal with him however I wish. Not to explain myself to you, madam."

"That isn't enough, in my view," Aunt Betsey said. "Raising a child is a serious responsibility."

"If you know so much about it, Miss Trotwood, then you do it. If David stays here, my door is shut to him forever."

"And what does David have to say?" My aunt turned to me. "Are you ready to go?"

I answered no, and begged her not to let me go. I said that the Murdstones had never liked me or been kind to me, that they had put themselves between my beloved mother and me, and that I feared them both.

"Mr. Bick," said my aunt, "what shall I do with this child?"

Mr. Bick looked at each of us in turn, hesitated, brightened, and said, "Have him measured for a suit of clothes."

"There you have it—wise advice as always from my dear friend," said Aunt Betsey, straightening to her full height. "Mr. Murdstone, I don't believe a word you've told me of David. And I know what kind of a life you gave his mother. I know it was a horrid day when you entered her life, when you set to training her, to breaking her spirit like a caged bird, to wearing away her life in teaching her to sing *your* tune. A tyrant—that's you! You broke your wife's heart and killed her as surely as if you'd shot her dead, but you won't hurt David anymore. Now, get out and take your sneering sister."

With that, Aunt Betsey took my hand and Mr. Bick's and led us from the parlor. We went to the kitchen and there, still holding our hands, she declared that she and Mr. Bick would have joint guardianship of me and that from then on she would call me Trotwood Copperfield ("Trot" for short) and we would all be a family.

It was several weeks later when my aunt asked, "Trot, would you like to go to school in the town of Canterbury? It's quite close to Dover and we can visit often."

I said I'd like it very much and by the next morning my clothes were packed. Aunt Betsey drove the pony cart herself and I sat beside her.

"Is it a large school, Aunt?" I asked.

"Don't know! We're going to visit Mr. Wickfield first and see what's available."

Mr. Wickfield practiced law in Canterbury, in a beautiful old house that seemed to lean out over the road. The place was spotlessly clean, with an old-fashioned brass doorknocker so well polished that it twinkled like a star.

The first person out the door when my aunt pulled the pony to a stop at the curb was a skeleton-thin young man whose bright red hair was cut almost to stubble. He had no visible eyebrows or eyelashes, and I wondered how his red-brown eyes, so unshaded, ever went to sleep. His bony, high-shouldered frame was dressed in good black cloth, and a long, thin hand extended from the sleeve that came forward to take the pony's reins from Aunt Betsey.

"Uriah Heep, is Mr. Wickfield at home?" asked my aunt.

"He is, ma'am," Heep replied, pointing his other long arm and skinny hand toward the house.

We went into an office and sat down with Mr. Wickfield. After introductions, Aunt Betsey told him why we'd come.

"We want a school where he'll be thoroughly taught and well-treated," she said.

"There's room for him to learn at the best one in town, but not room for him to live," Wickfield told us. "So, he could live here with us. It's quiet as a monastery, ideal for study."

While they completed the arrangements for my entering the school and taking residence with Mr. Wickfield, I went out into the hallway. At the end of the passage was a room and in the center of it I could see the red-haired man hunched over a desk, writing. As I moved closer to the room, I realized Heep's sleepless eyes, like two red suns, were staring up at me below his hairless brows. They never moved from me for the several moments I stood in the hallway, and I became so uncomfortable that I turned back to the office and went inside.

Mr. Wickfield took us to meet his daughter, Agnes, a girl of about my own age. Her face was bright and happy, and there was a calm about her that I have never forgotten.

We all had a light lunch that Agnes prepared and then Aunt Betsey and I went out to the pony cart to say our farewell.

"Trot, be a credit to yourself—never be dishonest, mean, or cruel, and you'll do well here. Mr. Bick and I will see you soon."

With that she hugged me quickly, got into the cart, and drove away.

Mr. Wickfield, Agnes, and I shared dinner and then went to the parlor where Agnes played piano while I watched the fire and Mr. Wickfield drank more red wine than I thought possible.

After Agnes went to her room, I wandered out into the street to get some air. When I came back I saw Uriah Heep locking the law office door. I was feeling so good about my life and friendly toward everyone that I offered him my hand in greeting. Oh, what a rude surprise it was! What a clammy hand, as ghostly to feel as to see! I rubbed mine after we parted, both to warm it and to rub off his touch.

The next morning, Mr. Wickfield took me to my new school, a huge stone building with a scholarly air about it. I met the headmaster, Dr. Strong, and was led by him to my classroom and introduced as "Trotwood Copperfield" to the twenty-five or thirty boys quietly engaged in study. And with that, the best years of my education began.

At dinner that evening, the Wickfields were eager to hear my impressions of the school and I assured them I liked it very much. Red wine for Mr. Wickfield, piano music by Agnes, and several games of dominoes followed our meal. Then I brought my schoolbooks down and Agnes gave me some ideas on the best ways to learn and understand everything the books contained.

It was getting late and there was very little wine left in Mr. Wickfield's decanter when I rose and said goodnight.

I wandered downstairs and saw a light under the office door. Uriah Heep held a sort of strange fascination for me. I went into the office where I found him reading a great, fat book with such apparent attention that his bony forefinger ran along every line as he read and, I imagined, made clammy snail-like tracks along the page.

"Working late, Uriah?" I asked.

"Yes, Master Copperfield. But not on office matters. I'm studying law," he explained.

I took a seat on a stool across the desk from him and made a show of opening my book to work while he went back to his labored reading. I studied him, noting that he often ground the palms of his hands against each other as if to squeeze them warm and dry.

"You must be quite a great lawyer," I mused after I'd watched him for a while.

"Me, Master Copperfield?" said Uriah. "Oh, no! I'm a very humble person—the humblest person around. My mother is the same, a very

humble person. We live in a humble house, Master Copperfield, but have much to be thankful for. My father was a humble man, too, rest his humble soul."

"Have you been with Mr. Wickfield a long time?" I asked.

"This is my fourth year. And grateful we are, my humble mother and I, that he would take me in and trouble himself to teach me and let me apprentice here. It would all be beyond my mother's humble means."

He had a way of wiggling when he was enthusiastic about something—a way that was very ugly indeed, full of snaky twistings of his throat and body.

"And when your studies are over, you'll be a regular lawyer and maybe a partner in the firm?"

"Oh, no," Uriah assured me, "I'm much too humble for that."

At last he rose and closed the heavy book. "Mother will be expecting me," he said, "and she'll be getting uneasy with my lateness. We are much attached to one another, Master Copperfield."

We walked across the dark hall. He shook my hand—his fingers like small, squirmy fish in the dark—and crept out through a very slim opening of the door.

I shuddered and went up to the protective haven of my room.

Within two weeks from that first day in class, I was quite at home with my school and my schoolmates. It was an excellent place, as different from Mr. Creakle's school as good is from evil, with an appeal to every boy's honor and good faith in all things, and each of us felt we had a part in sustaining its character and dignity. Surrounded by my new, much-improved fortune, the Murdstone and Grinby life fell away behind so that I hardly believed it had ever happened. My new life grew so familiar it seemed I had been leading it for a very long time.

CHAPTER 6

Somebody Turns Up

O n my way to class one Monday morning, I met Uriah in the street. He invited me to come to his home to meet his mother and share tea with them.

I said I wanted to ask Mr. Wickfield's permission, and if he approved, I'd meet Uriah in the law office at six o'clock.

"Mother will be proud, indeed," Uriah said. "Or she would be proud, if it wasn't sinful, you understand."

At six o'clock, we left Mr. Wickfield's and walked the several blocks to the Heep residence. Mrs. Heep met us in a low-ceilinged, old-fashioned room, half parlor and half kitchen, that opened directly off the street and, in fact, was connected to the street by a doorway wider by half than any such entry I'd ever seen. Uriah pushed the large door all the way back on its hinges, and left it full open.

Uriah was the perfect image of his mother, only taller. And they shared the same view of themselves and their existence: everything was humble and much too insignificant to be worth the notice of another living soul.

"This is a day to be remembered, my Uriah, I am sure," said Mrs. Heep, pouring cups of tea all around, "when the fine Master Copperfield pays us a visit."

I was embarrassed by the compliments but took them not so much for their truth as for their intention to make me feel welcome.

"My Uriah has looked forward to this day for a long while," she assured me. "He feared that our humbleness stood in the way, and I joined in those fears myself. Humble we are, humble we have been, humble we shall always be," said Mrs. Heep.

We drank our tea and spoke casually of Canterbury and of the unusually cool evenings we'd been having. Then they began to talk about aunts, and I told them about mine; and about fathers and mothers, and I told them about mine; and Mrs. Heep spoke about stepfathers, and I began to tell her about mine, but stopped because my aunt had advised me to keep silent about the Murdstones.

A tender young tooth would have had no more defense against a pair of dentists than I had against Uriah and his mother. They did just what they liked with me, worming out bits of information that I had no desire to tell. The skill with which one followed up whatever the other said was a touch of art. And I was not prepared to resist it.

I had become uncomfortable with my visit and rose to end it, walking to the gaping doorway and preparing to say my farewells to the

Heeps, when a man stepped over from the street, exclaiming loudly, "Copperfield, can it be you?"

It was Mr. Micawber.

"Copperfield, this is extraordinary!" he cried. "I was just telling myself that something would turn up, and here you are, out of the blue!"

There was no way to avoid introducing the Heeps and Mr. Micawber.

"Any friend of David's has a claim on my heart, too," he told Uriah and his mother.

"We are too humble, sir, for your attentions," said Mrs. Heep.

I was anxious to take my leave from the Heeps and so I suggested we go at once to see Mrs. Micawber. We walked a few streets over to a boardinghouse and went upstairs. Mrs. Micawber was amazed but glad to see me, and we sat down to talk while her husband left to check the job notices in that day's newspaper.

"I thought you were in Plymouth," I said.

"We were but the local influence of my family was of no use in getting any employment for my husband," she told me. "In fact, our reception was quite cool."

She said they'd had no choice but to sell what they owned—even the prized walking

stick—to pay for transportation back to London, and seek some way of making a living there again. They would be leaving Canterbury at week's end.

I felt so very badly for the Micawbers, and said I wished I could help in any way, but she assured me that my friendship was help enough, and Mr. Micawber, returning with no employment in sight, told me he knew something would turn up soon and I shouldn't worry about them.

It was early the next morning when I saw the disturbing sight of Mr. Micawber and Uriah Heep walking together. And when I asked him about it several days later, Micawber was glad to say, "Your friend Heep is a young fellow who will go very far in the study of law, David. If I had known him at the time when my difficulties came to a crisis, things would have been a great deal better managed than they were."

He told me he'd been pleased to share a drink with Uriah and his mother the evening after I had introduced them, and that a lovely time was had by all. I didn't want to ask if the Heeps had questioned him about me, or if he had offered any information, but alarms rang in my head at the thought of those two dealing with a tongue loosened by brandy. The Heeps seemed set on gathering information for some unhealthy purpose.

CHAPTER 7

Out of School
and Into the World

I would have trouble saying whether I was glad or sad when my five years at Canterbury school came to a close. At 17, I was reasonably expected to make some worthwhile place for myself in the world. Such grand and misty ideas I had about the glamour of being a young man abroad in the world, making my own decisions, going my own way, turning society to the better by my presence!

I'd gone home to Dover after graduation, to relax, to enjoy the company of Aunt Betsey and Mr. Bick, and to figure out what I was going to do next. After a dozen or more serious conversations about my future, my aunt suggested I might gain some clearer view of what I wanted if I had a temporary change of scene. She thought a trip to the sea at Yarmouth and some time spent with Peggotty and her family might be just the answer.

I went first to Canterbury to say good-bye to Agnes and Mr. Wickfield, and to pack the books and clothing still left in my room there. In the last few moments before I boarded the coach for London, while we had some time alone, I told Agnes how strange it felt not to see her every evening, not to have her wise advice on every subject and her gentle sense of fun that kept all of life in a clearer perspective.

"I'm worried about my father, Trotwood ... especially now that you're leaving," she said. "Have you noticed the change in him, a gradual change over these years? What is it?"

I'd seen that his hands shook and his words were sometimes hard to make out. I believed it was the result of the decanters of red wine he drank, and I told Agnes that.

"What worries me most," she said, "is that whenever he is in his worst condition, Uriah comes to him for some business matter that has to be worked on right that moment. Knowing he's performed poorly, he feels that much worse, and so he drinks that much more the next day. And again Uriah comes for him. Father relies on Heep more and more now that you're not here to keep him company."

Uriah and Mr. Wickfield came to say my trunk had been stashed on the coach and the driver was impatient to leave. Agnes and I hugged farewell, Mr. Wickfield told me I would always be welcome in his home, and Uriah slipped the chill-skinned bones of his hand into mine for one last, unpleasant shake. Then I was off to Yarmouth and the sea.

We took the Dover Road to London, the same road I'd walked and slept beside five years before, and arrived at a hotel in Charing Cross in late afternoon. I was resolved to act older and more polished than I really felt, and to do only grown-up things, so I attended a performance of *Julius Caesar* at the Covent Garden Theater. When I returned to the hotel, I was still caught up in its excitement, and much too awake for bed. I went instead to the coffee-room and sat watching the fire and recalling the play until long past one a.m.

I don't know when I first noticed the handsome young man who sat reading on the leather sofa across the room. I passed him with a quick glance, then stopped, and looked back. No, could it be? I stepped across the carpet and stood looking at him.

"Steerforth? James Steerforth, is it you?" I asked in not much more than a whisper.

He looked at me and I could tell he hadn't a clue who I might be.

"I'm afraid you don't—Zot! It's little Copperfield, isn't it?" he suddenly exclaimed and rose to shake my hand.

"I never, never, never was so glad, Steerforth! I'm overjoyed to see you," I gushed.

"Whoa, Copperfield, old boy, don't overdo it!" But he seemed pleased to see how meeting him affected me.

I told him quickly why I was in the hotel, and asked what had brought him there.

"Well, I'm at Oxford College now, and I'm going to visit my mother. The roads are in awful condition this time of year and our house is boring, so I stopped here and wasted my evening at a dreadful play at Covent."

I had no reason to tell him how I'd loved the play—my maturity and, therefore, worth were on the line.

"So, tell me what you're doing," he urged me. "Where are you going and what's in your future?"

When I explained the purpose of my travel to Yarmouth, and the lack of any distinct vision of my future, he suggested I join him for a day or two at his mother's house in the London suburb of Highgate.

"She's a little vain and boring about me, Copperfield, but she'll like you a lot," he said. "She likes anyone who likes me."

It was dusk when the coach left us at an old brick house on the summit of a hill in Highgate. Steerforth's mother hurried out to meet us—to meet Steerforth, that is. We were all well into the front hallway before she even noticed I was there, dragging in his trunks and cases.

When I was introduced, she hugged me, too, and said she'd heard her son speak of the little lad who thought him the bravest and brightest at the school, and she could tell I was a smart boy myself to have recognized her son's great value.

We all sat together in the afternoon, my friend, his mother, and her companion Rosa Dartle—a sharp-angled woman with a large scar along her upper lip. When I later asked Steerforth about that scar, he said, "I did it."

"It must have been an unfortunate accident," I exclaimed.

"Not really. I was a youngster and she did something that made me angry, so I threw a hammer at her. I suppose I wasn't an angel of a child."

I found there was no end to Mrs. Steerforth's devotion to her son. She seemed able to think or speak of nothing else, and turned every subject to one angle or another until it somehow focused itself on James. After supper, she showed me pictures of his infancy, and locks of his hair. She brought out grade reports from his years at Salem House. She was about to begin a reading of all the letters he'd ever written her, when Steerforth put an end to it.

"Copperfield is going to the sea, Mother. To Yarmouth," he said.

"I'm going to see a dear old friend who lived with my mother and me in Blunderstone," I told them. "And to see her brother and his family. Daniel Peggotty, remember, Steerforth? You met him once at school."

"He had his son with him, right? A big lump of a boy."

"His nephew, Ham," I corrected. "He also has a niece, Em'ly. Ham and Em'ly aren't related, except by being orphaned at young ages and both being adopted into Daniel's big heart. The countryside 'round Yarmouth is full of people who've known his generosity and kindness. He's a remarkable man. Why don't you come to Yarmouth with me, and meet him again?"

"What an idea! It would be worth the journey just to see how people like that live," Steerforth said with a smile.

I was wondering what "people like that" meant when Miss Dartle asked directly, "Are they really animals and clods, those people who live in the country and by the water?"

"There's a wide separation between them and us, Rosa," was Steerforth's indifferent response. "They're not sensitive like us, not so easily shocked. And like their coarse, rough skins, they're not readily wounded."

I believed my friend had said all this as a joke, but no one laughed and none of them disputed his words.

In the week I spent at Highgate, Steerforth's servant Littimer was often and discreetly present at most of our activities. He got horses for us, and Steerforth, who knew how to do everything, gave me lessons in riding. He brought us slim swords and Steerforth taught me something of fencing. He produced gloves and Steerforth improved my boxing.

At week's end, Steerforth decided to go to Yarmouth with me, but to leave the always-helpful Littimer at Highgate. I wasn't disappointed that he wouldn't be going along because I couldn't shake the feeling that Littimer was not as respectable as he appeared.

Steerforth and I spent the first night of our seaside visit at a local inn because the coach had arrived too late for us to present ourselves to Peggotty and Barkis or to Daniel and his household. In the morning, I led him around

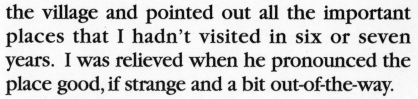

the village and pointed out all the important places that I hadn't visited in six or seven years. I was relieved when he pronounced the place good, if strange and a bit out-of-the-way.

"And when are you off to your friend Peggotty's, Davy?" he asked, when we turned back toward the inn.

"Now, James. I want to surprise her and Barkis. Will you come along?"

"I think I'll miss the squeals and tears of renewed friendship if you don't mind, Davy," my companion laughed. "But I'll be glad to join you later."

I drew him a crude map to Peggotty's house, then waved good-bye and walked to the Barkis cottage.

Although Peggotty and I had kept in touch almost weekly by letter, we hadn't seen one another in nearly seven years. Those years had brought big changes in my appearance, and when she opened the door to me, I could see no hint of recognition on her face.

"Peggotty!" I cried to her. "You look just the same as ever."

There was still another moment of uncertainty before she leapt a foot straight up into the air, flinging her arms open and squealing, "Davy, Davy, my darling boy, Davy!" loud enough to be heard several houses downwind.

We hugged and spun around, laughing and crying, and when I lifted her off her sturdy legs high into the air, some of her tears splashed on my nose and the top of my head. Never before and never since have I had such a welcome in any place.

When we'd gotten some control of ourselves and gone into her kitchen, Peggotty told me Barkis was seldom out of bed, his health being so poor, but that he'd be cheered by the sight of me—and so he was, for we sat with him at least an hour and we talked about those early trips from The Rookery to Yarmouth.

It wasn't long until Steerforth popped up at the door. His easy-spirited good humor and handsome looks won Peggotty completely. We stayed on for dinner and Steerforth was the star, charming our hosts with stories of their wonderful Davy at Salem House.

We left the cottage in the early evening and walked over the dark, wintry sands to Daniel's boat-house. The wind wailed around us more mournfully than I had ever heard.

"This is a wild kind of place, isn't it?" I asked.

"Dismal enough in the dark," he said, "and the sea roars like it is hungry for us."

Daniel and his family were not expecting us.

"Mas'r Davy! It's Mas'r Davy!" Ham and Daniel shouted to Em'ly and several neighbor women who looked at us in astonishment. The men bounded across the floor to clap me on the back and tug me into the room.

"Why, if this ain't the brightest night of my life," cried Daniel, "I'm a boiled shellfish!"

Everyone spoke at once, me introducing Steerforth, them introducing the neighbors, me explaining we'd just been to see Peggotty, them saying they were toasting the coming wedding of Ham and Em'ly.

Again my capacity for surprise was tested. Ham and Em'ly—why, I'd never imagined such a pairing. But when Ham took the floor to say to all of us just how much the darling girl meant to him and how strongly he pledged to protect and love her all his life, they seemed the ideal couple.

Into all of this merriment, Steerforth fit perfectly. He joined in the toasting and the well-wishing as if these folks were lifelong friends, listening with quiet respect to Daniel's ramblings about his dreams for his adopted children's futures, and charming the neighbor ladies with somewhat naughty tales of life in London.

Em'ly, shy and untraveled and yearning to be more than all she saw around her, sat by the fire fascinated by Steerforth, the handsome visitor from a place she'd never been and feared she'd never go. She smiled at him when he smiled at her, and laughed at his stories, and watched him intensely with a look I might then have taken for wonder but that now I know was the first step toward despair.

We stayed on in Yarmouth for two weeks. I spent much of my time with Peggotty and Barkis, returning each night to the room they kept for me. Steerforth went boating with

Daniel most days. I'd stop at Daniel's each evening to share the news of the day with him and Em'ly and Ham, and then Steerforth and I would walk into town for dinner and conversation at the local pub.

One windy night I found Steerforth alone in Daniel's boat-house, sitting so lost in his thoughts before the fire that my greeting all but knocked him off his chair.

"Have I called you down from the stars?" I asked him.

"No," he answered, "nowhere so lofty as that. I was looking at the pictures in the fire." He took a piece of burning wood and quickly stirred the flames, as if the act could remove the faces he saw there and keep me from seeing those same things.

We said nothing for several minutes.

"Copperfield," he said quietly, "a loving mother is a gift, but I could have used a father to guide me better into manhood. And I wish for all the world that I could do a better job of guiding myself through it now. It would be better to be poor Daniel or big, lumpy Ham than to be James Steerforth, twenty times richer and twenty times smarter. I'm a torment to myself, and I'm a torment to others."

There was nothing I could say, so deep was his unhappiness.

"I'm heavy company for myself sometimes," he mused. "What old women call 'the horrors'

123

have been creeping over me this evening ... I've become afraid of myself." He straightened and gave a little laugh. "But, enough of this gloom! Must we abandon this buccaneer life tomorrow, Davy? I wish there was nothing to do but toss about on the sea."

"You'd only wish that until the novelty wore off, James," I said, teasing.

"You're right! I tire quickly of just about everything," he agreed. "Did I tell you I've bought a boat? It was an impulse, perhaps, but when I'm not here Daniel will keep it and use it in place of that rotted tub of his. She's being repainted and made ship-shape now. And she'll be renamed 'The Little Em'ly.' "

At once I marveled at my friend and at the natural generosity that had prompted a purchase that would be such a help to Daniel. What kind of monsters hid in his heart to frighten him of himself?

When I returned to Peggotty's house later that evening, Ham was sitting on the front steps.

"Anything wrong, Ham? Is it Barkis?" I asked.

"It's Em'ly. She's talking to someone inside."

"Who is it?"

"A young woman she knew from school, Martha. Pretty pitiful creature she is, too. We, Em'ly and I, were out walking this evening just before the wind came up so wild, and we heard a woman's voice calling out to Em'ly for help. 'Have a woman's heart to help me,' she cried, over and over. Clear she's been living a hard time at the waterside, with the sailors and the boatboys. One eye's been blackened and there are bruises old and new on her arms. Em'ly couldn't take her to Daniel's place—it would have upset him too much to see her with his beloved Em'ly—so we brought her here."

Just then Peggotty opened the cottage door to call Ham inside, and motioned me along, too. Em'ly spoke first: "Martha wants to go to London."

"Why to London?" asked Ham.

125

"Because she knows no one there," Em'ly said.

"If you'll help me get there, I'll try to make a better go of it than I have here. Please help me get off these streets!"

Em'ly rose and went to Ham. "Can we help her?" she asked in a whisper.

Ham took a little canvas bag from his jacket pocket and poured its few silver coins into her hand. "It's yours, Em'ly, to use as you want. Everything I have on earth is yours," he said.

Em'ly returned to Martha and sat beside her, talking softly for some minutes. Then the women stood and walked to the door. Martha gripped Em'ly's hand. "God bless the goodness of you and your fine people," she said, looking at each of us in turn, then closed the door behind her.

At once, Em'ly began to cry, deep and clawing sobs shaking her so that Ham picked her up and placed her on the cushioned sofa.

"Don't cry, my Em'ly," he soothed. "Don't cry so, darlin'."

"Ham!" she exclaimed, still crying pitifully. "I'm not as good a person as I should be! I'm not as thankful as I have every reason to be.

"I'm mean to you, Ham. I know it. And I'm moody and cross and ungrateful for your love, when others have not a moment of love in their lives or any strong arm to help them stand."

"Em'ly," Ham exclaimed, "I'm happy every day just to think of you, just to see you!"

"That's because *you're* good, not because I am. It would have been wiser for you to have fallen in love with someone better than I, Ham, someone not vain, someone as bound to you as you are to me."

All of Em'ly's suffering was too much for Peggotty. "Wisdom has not much to do with love, Em'ly," she said, sitting down beside her and gathering her into a hug. "We love whom we love, and we do the best we can at it. None of us is ever as good as we could be, or should be. We give and take our love as a kind of grace."

Peggotty's embrace calmed Em'ly's sobs, and we all took our turn at coaxing her, by degrees, back into a lighter mood. When she was at last able to smile and then to laugh, Ham led her to the door and I watched them walk down the path, Em'ly with both hands holding Ham's large arm and leaning in close against the wind.

We left the seaside next morning. We departed to the regret of a good many friends, old and new, making promises to return soon with every backward wave.

For some time we didn't talk. I sat wondering how long it would be until I would see those dear faces again, and Steerforth engaged in his own musings.

"So, Davy, at breakfast you mentioned a letter from your aunt," Steerforth broke through my thoughts. "Not bad news, I hope."

"She reminds me that I came out on this expedition to take a look around and think about what I'm going to do with my life."

"Have you done so?" he asked.

"Not at all! To tell the truth, I'd forgotten all about it."

"Well, look about you now and decide," he laughed as he stuck his head out the carriage windows, first left and then right. "Bad news, my friend. There's nothing much out there but flat meadow beside boggy swamp."

"Not very promising unless I'm meant to be a wildflower or a crocodile," I said. "Aunt Betsey has suggested a career as a civil attorney."

"Dry stuff, Davy. Nowhere as interesting as criminal law, but very respectable and well paid. All in all, not a bad idea."

"My aunt is coming in from Dover to meet me and she has a law firm in mind where I could apprentice. We'll go and have a look," I said.

Steerforth and I said our good-byes at the coach office and I met my aunt for dinner at Lincoln's Inn.

We were finishing our dessert when she said, "Well, Trot, what do you think of the civil attorney plan?"

"I've thought of it and talked it over with Steerforth, and I like it!" I exclaimed. "I like it a great deal, in fact. But won't my apprenticeship cost a great deal of money?"

"It will cost a thousand pounds, Trot."

"You've already spent so much on my education, and everything else I've needed you've supplied. Are you certain you want to spend another huge sum?"

"If I have any object in my life, Trot," my aunt said, "it's to provide for your being a good, sensible, and happy man. And if this career leads to that, no more can I ask."

"Then let's go and see the firm you've thought of first thing tomorrow, and I can get to work," I said.

The offices of Spenlow and Jorkins were in Doctors' Commons, set in such a way under a series of arches and around a few twists of a side road that although it was in the heart of London, the sound of the great city was much muted there.

Mr. Spenlow called us into his private room. He was a tiny, white-haired man wearing the stiffest collar I had ever seen. The stiffness seemed to stretch the entire length of his body for he never sat, and when he moved, it was as one piece. When he bent to look at papers on his desk, he seemed to bend from the shoes forward.

"Do you wish a career in civil law, Copperfield?" he asked. "Wills and marriage agreements and Acts of Parliament are the stuff of our days, you know. Not much romance in it."

I told him I thought it would suit me well, but that I hoped there would be a period during which I could try it and see if I wished to continue.

"Quite so! We always have a month's initiation. If you don't want to continue, there is no financial obligation. How does that sound?"

Aunt Betsey and Mr. Spenlow concluded the necessary arrangements and we settled on my beginning my month's probation the following Monday. Then we spent the balance of the afternoon looking for a comfortable boardinghouse in the neighborhood where I could be close to the offices. When my aunt shared her worries about how Mr. Bick was faring back in Dover, I urged her to go home and look after him as soon as she could, assuring her that I was then much better prepared for life in London than I had been the first time there.

Two days after my aunt left for Dover, and the day after I began to make myself at home in Mrs. Crupp's boardinghouse near Doctors' Commons, a messenger brought a note from Agnes. She had written to say she was in London at the home of her father's friend Mr.

Waterbrook, and needed to speak with me as soon as possible. I ran my housekeeping errands and was on her doorstep at four o'clock.

How good it was to see her! She asked to hear all about my trip to the sea, and she wanted news of my upcoming apprenticeship. When at last she asked if I had seen Uriah Heep since I'd been in London, I knew we had come to the serious reason for her visit.

"Heep?" I asked. "In London?"

"He comes to Mr. Waterbrook's office almost every week—on disagreeable business, Trotwood. I believe he is going to enter into partnership with my father."

"No! Don't tell me that worm has wiggled himself into such a promotion," I exclaimed, disgusted and unable to imagine that Mr. Wickfield could be such a fool.

"You recall our conversation about the changes in Papa?" Agnes asked. "It wasn't more than two or three days after that when Uriah told my father he was going to have to look elsewhere for a better job. He's convinced Papa that he's needed, mostly by setting up business situations when Papa is not well and then seeming to rescue the dealings after Papa has bungled things. My father is afraid of losing Uriah's help and he persuaded him to stay by offering the partnership. Uriah claims to be humble and grateful, but it's he who has the power over my father, and he makes a hard use of it."

"Agnes, you can't permit this. You've got to change your father's mind!"

"It's no use, Trotwood. Papa loves me dearly, but he fears himself and he fears Uriah—and in this case that fear is stronger than love. And I must ask you, Trotwood, to be friendly with Uriah, for our sake. Don't repel him for he may take it out on Papa, and mistreat him even more severely."

I was invited to a dinner party the next evening at the Waterbrook's home. Among the guests was Uriah Heep, dressed in a black suit and a maddening air of deep humility. He stood close to me all evening, and whenever I spoke to Agnes his shadowless eyes followed us and he leaned in slightly to hear our words.

Balancing the irritation I felt from Heep's presence was my joy in another unexpected guest—Tommy Traddles! I heard him loudly introduced to an old couple at the far end of the dining table and asked my host if that could be the same Traddles I'd known at Salem

House, the honorable but unlucky little fidget who drew page after page of skeletons and frequently ran sadly against Mr. Creakle's whip.

"Could surely be the one," Waterbrook laughed. "He's a good fellow. Nobody's enemy but his own. He's studying law at present."

Traddles and I met a bit later on the stairway, both of us marveling at the timing that would put us at one man's table on the same night. Heep, of course, stood near and I had no choice but to introduce him to my old friend. He wiggled with such excitement and declared his humbleness so strongly that I wanted to throw him over the railing.

When very few guests remained, I said good-night to my hosts. There were footsteps behind me on the porch and I turned to find Heep wrapping a woolen scarf around his long neck as he followed me into the street. I was in no mood for his company but, mindful of Agnes' request that I treat him well, I invited him home for coffee.

"Don't feel you have to open your home to someone as humble as me, Mister Copperfield," was his oily response as he hung close beside me to my boardinghouse.

There were no lights on in the house and I took his hand to lead him up the dark stairs so he wouldn't trip or knock his head against anything. His damp, cold hand was like a fistful of frog and I was tempted to drop it and run.

When I'd poured his coffee and he'd protested my serving him in the face of his being much too humble for such service, he said slyly, "I suppose you've heard of the change in my position with Mr. Wickfield."

I said I had.

"You're a prophet, Copperfield. Do you remember telling me once I might become a partner in Mr. Wickfield's business? Wickfield and Heep, you said then."

He sat with the jack-o-lantern grin carved into his face, looking at the fire as I looked at him.

"I recall mentioning it, Heep, but I never thought it would happen," I said.

"Nor I, sir, nor I! But even the humblest person can be of help to another. And that has truly been the case for me. Mr. Wickfield is a fine man, but he's not been in good control of the business lately."

"And you are only stepping forward to assist him, to see that his interests are protected, is that it, Heep?" I struggled to keep the dis-

belief out of my voice. What a job it was for Agnes' sake!

"If anyone else had been in my place during the last few years, he could easily have had Mr. Wickfield under his thumb. There would have been loss, disgrace, and more. But I've helped to keep all of that away and he wishes to reward me beyond anything I could have dreamed."

"You must be very proud of the honor, Heep," I said.

"I've risen from my humble station, sir, but I am humble still. And I hope never to be anything but humble. May I tell you something and know that you will keep it just between us, Mister Copperfield?" He took out a handkerchief and wiped his palms slowly. "Humble as I am, humble as my mother is, Miss Agnes has been in my heart for years. I love the ground she walks on!"

I had a crazy notion of seizing the red-hot fireplace poker and putting an end to him the

minute Agnes' name was out of his mouth.
How could someone so slimy, so false, lay any
claim to love? How could he imagine such a
match?

"Have you told Agnes how you feel, Heep?" I
clung to some small control of myself.

"Oh no, indeed! I'm in no hurry. Agnes is
young. I think I have time to let her see how
useful I am to her father, and how I care for
his interests. She'll become familiar with my
hopes and, in time, I believe she'll see me as
the right partner for her, too."

Neither of us spoke for quite some time.
When finally Heep rose and begged my pardon for keeping me up so late, I was more
than glad to see him go. And although the
night was bitterly cold, I opened the windows
in the room where we had sat to freshen the
air and rid me of his presence.

CHAPTER 8

New Love and Old Friends

Days and weeks slipped by. During my probation at Spenlow and Jorkins I found I liked the work, and was apprenticed. To celebrate the occasion, Mr. Spenlow invited me to spend the weekend at his country house in Norwood. At the end of the workday on Friday, he and I drove to Norwood in his carriage. We talked of civil law and the courts and the general direction Parliament seemed to be moving, and the trip passed quickly.

The house—a large, white-brick place with perfectly cut gardens clustered with trees and brick walks—was welcoming, cheerfully lighted and colorfully decorated in the rich style of a hunting estate.

Mr. Spenlow was a widowed father of one daughter who had just finished her education in Paris and returned home. He called to his daughter as soon as we entered the hallway. I had just handed my coat to the butler and turned toward the stairs when my life's course was forever altered by his words: "Mr. Copperfield, my daughter Dora."

Yes. One word was all I could think. Yes.

In an instant she was all the world to me—I was swallowed up in a flood of love. There was no pausing on the brink, no looking down into the current, no glancing back. I was gone, head first, with no hope, no desire for rescue.

At Spenlow's urging, I went upstairs to unpack and dress for dinner, but spent the time instead sitting on the edge of my bed chewing on my luggage key and thinking of Dora—bright-eyed, lovely Dora.

I'm sure we had dinner. I know there were other people there. But who they were and what we ate I cannot say. I only remember sitting beside Dora, enjoying her rich voice and warm laugh. When she tapped my arm to ask if the untouched food didn't suit me, I shivered so badly my coffee sloshed down the front of my starched white shirt.

I couldn't sleep that night and was up before the birds. The garden walks were wet with dew, cool and misty. I hadn't been walking there long, thinking of where my heart had gone and what I was to do without it, when I turned a corner and met her.

I stuttered some silly greeting. "Isn't this a fresh morning?" she asked. "I love this time of day best of all." And again I fumbled for words.

We spoke a few more moments. Then she moved on around the corner to continue her walk and I retreated to my room to curse myself for my lack of grace.

In general, the weekend was quiet. Mr. Spenlow and I spent time reading in his library. All of our meals and teatimes we shared with Dora and by our return on Sunday evening, I had gotten myself enough in shape to be making intelligent conversation. Neither my host nor his daughter had any idea that I was hopelessly in love.

In the weeks after my time at Norwood, I found reasons to be out of the office, delivering papers or answering requests for meetings. And on rare occasions I saw Dora; several times we met by chance and talked. But I could never bring myself to tell her of my interest, let alone my slavish devotion. And I waited for another invitation to Mr. Spenlow's house—but none came.

I was in a rut, and decided to find other entertainment, so I called on Tommy Traddles. He lived on a little street near the Veterinary College at Camden Town. Something about the neighborhood—its shabbiness, the ten-

ants' habit of tossing unwanted things into the street and leaving them to rust or rot, the noise—reminded me of the places I'd lived with the Micawbers. The man delivering milk was shouting at the housekeeper when I walked up on the porch.

"Now, what of that bill of mine, eh? When will it be paid?"

"The master, he says he'll pay it right away, he does, sir," the young woman said. She was holding the pints of milk and packs of cheese tight in her arms.

"Do you like that milk you're clutching there? Because it's the last you'll taste until the bill is paid up. You tell the master that, will ya?" He rattled the empty bottles and stomped off to his wagon.

I stepped inside and was directed to a room at the top of the back stairs. Traddles was studying from a huge book, surrounded by even larger books and dictionaries on a table spilling over with papers.

We talked for a long time, recalling times at Salem House, catching up on where we'd been and what we'd done since. He told me of his studying for the bar examination, of his friends, and of his engagement to a minister's daughter.

"I'm saving every cent for the time we marry," he laughed, "because she's one of ten children and life is likely to be expensive! That's why I'm boarding here with the Micawbers. They have seen a good deal of life and are excellent company!"

"The who?" I exclaimed. *"Who* are your landlords?"

"The Micawbers. Fine people, although he seems unable to get a handle on a good job right now. Their luck's a little thin."

When I told Traddles how I knew the Micawbers, he insisted on running downstairs and asking them to join us.

"Good heavens, Traddles," cried Mr. Micawber as he pumped my arm with all his might, "to think that you should know my favorite boy, Copperfield! It's a small world, indeed."

We had more catching up to do. More news of Micawber's endless waiting for something to turn up and the money-losing schemes he concocted in the meantime. More words of support from his long-suffering wife. The evening was dark and the fire all but burned out when I rose to leave.

The next evening my landlady brought word that a very handsome and well-dressed man was waiting for me in the parlor. Steerforth, I thought at once.

"Can it be, Davy, that I've caught you in?" he cried. "I expected the busy young lawyer to be out playing the fool with any of a cast of young women! Are you only taking an evening's rest? Why, you Doctors' Commons fellows are the most social men in London."

"We're a wild crowd, James!" I laughed at the thought. "If you consider green eyeshades and suspenders partywear! And so how is life at Oxford — all somber study, I'm sure."

"Don't know that," he said. "I've been in Yarmouth the last couple weeks, checking on my boat and generally having a good time. The Little Em'ly is quite a nice bit of work."

"How is everyone there? Is Em'ly married yet?"

"Not yet. Probably will be soon, though." He picked up his coat and slid a hand into the inside pocket. "I've got a letter for you, from your friend Peggotty. Old what's-his-name's in a bad way."

"Do you mean Barkis?" I made my way through Peggotty's curly, wavy-lined script and folded the letter again.

"It's tough," Steerforth said as he pulled on his coat and scarf, "but the sun sets every day and people die every minute. We can't be frightened by someone else's death. No! Ride on over all obstacles and win the race at any price! That's the lesson for me."

I put on my coat and walked with him to the end of the lane. We said good night and he turned away toward the carriage stand, then stopped and came back. He stood a moment, studying the gloves he held in his left hand, then looked at me.

"Davy, if anything should ever separate us, you have to think of me at my best. Let's make that a deal. Think of me at my best, if circumstances ever part us!"

He turned away again, and with long strides he was around the corner in a moment. Watching him go, I thought of his saying, "Ride on over all obstacles and win the race!" and I wished, for the first time, that he had some race worth running.

CHAPTER 9

Losses and a Search

T he next morning I explained to Mr. Spenlow that I needed a few days away to visit a dying friend, and left at noon for Yarmouth. I took a room at the hotel because it was late evening when the coach pulled into the village. At ten o'clock I went out for an evening's walk, to fill myself with the smell of the sea and think of my dear friend Peggotty and of Barkis, whose quiet, countrified ways I would miss.

Then I walked the few blocks to Peggotty's cottage. Daniel answered my soft tap at the front door. Em'ly was sitting by the fire with her face in her hands, Ham beside her.

I heard their news of Barkis and of Peggotty spoken in whispers. Everyone was subdued, given the presence of Death in the house, but Em'ly most of all. She seemed to be a vapor, a mist, less than present, drained of all the usual color in her cheeks and eyes—pale, almost transparent, and filled with tears.

Peggotty came down from Barkis' bedside because she said she'd heard my voice. She hugged me and I felt her shaking. "Come up with me, Davy," she said. "Barkis has always loved and admired you."

We went up the stairs and I stood beside the old cart driver. His eyes didn't open, his fingers lay still, and there was barely any movement of his chest under the cover.

Daniel came into the room and stood beside me. "He's goin' out with the tide," he whispered.

"With the tide?"

"People along the seacoast can't die until the tide's out. Can't be born unless it's in, either. He's waiting for the tide to go."

We stayed by Barkis' bed for hours. At the end he opened his eyes, searching for Peggotty; he lightly squeezed my hand, and died.

I saw Daniel glance at the clock on the bed table. "Tide's out," he said.

There was not much ceremony for Barkis' burial. He was taken to Blunderstone and placed in the graveyard beside The Rookery. I stayed on in Yarmouth to attend to his will.

During the days after the funeral I saw nothing of Em'ly, but Daniel told me she was to be married quietly in two weeks. Peggotty and I made arrangements to leave for London where we would file the will and estate papers with the court.

Rain was falling heavily the night before our trip. Wind howled in off the sea and splashed the windows. When the rain slowed to a drizzle and the moon came out I slogged across the wet sand to the boat-house to say good-bye to Daniel and Ham and Em'ly. The house was bright and warm, fire blazing, pipe smoke scenting the air around Daniel. Peggotty was there, sewing. But there was no Em'ly and no Ham. I sat and watched the fire peacefully with sister and brother, feeling the old kinship of years before.

Not ten minutes had passed when Ham came through the door, looking storm-tossed and pale, wet to the skin.

"Where's Em'ly?" asked Daniel.

Ham made a movement with his head that seemed to mean she was outside. "Davy, will you come out a moment and see what we have to show you?" he asked me.

He pulled me into the open air and closed the door behind him. Em'ly was not there.

"What's wrong?" I asked.

He began to cry, broken-hearted wails and gasps were all he could produce. No words. No answers. I didn't know what to do in the face of such grief. I could only look at him and repeat my question.

"She's gone, Davy. She's run away! What am I going to do? What am I going to say to Daniel? You know how he loves her!"

I was standing with my back to the rain, facing Ham and the front door. There was no time to reach around the sobbing man and grip the handle when I saw the door start to open. Daniel thrust his head toward us.

"Where is she, Ham? What's happened to my little girl?" he asked with a look of fear that I had never seen the equal of.

We went inside and Ham read from a note Em'ly had left for him.

"'When you see this, I will be far away,'" he began. "'Tell Uncle Daniel that I loved him, and that my heart is torn to leave this way. Love some good woman, Ham—one who will love you as much as you love me. God bless you all.'"

The reading was slow and difficult for Ham. Everyone sat looking at him for a moment when he finished.

Ham raised his head and looked at me. "I don't want you to think I blame you at all, Davy. It wasn't your doin' that Em'ly left us."

I felt the stab of truth in my belly. "Who has she gone away with?" I asked, already certain I knew the answer.

"Mr. Omer said he saw a strange carriage in town this morning, and in it a man he'd seen at the boatyards several times. Another man, Omer said a servant of some sort, made two trips to and from the carriage, both times carrying boxes and bags, and the second time

Em'ly was with him. She got into the carriage, and all rode away. By the way Omer spoke of the man in the carriage, I know it was James Steerforth, and his man Littimer."

Daniel walked to the bank of coats and scarves hanging inside the door, and took his rough jacket from its peg at the end. Ham asked where he was going.

"I'm going to find her. First I'm going to sink that boat of his—The Little Em'ly, he called it! Then I'm going to find her—and I won't rest until I know she's safe, whether here or somewhere else."

Ham stepped over beside the door. "Daniel, the baggage man heard Littimer tell the driver they were going to London and then across the Channel to France."

"They're well into London and may already have sailed for the Continent," I said.

"I won't be stopped!" Daniel exclaimed. "Whether I begin now or tomorrow, no difference. I won't quit until I find her. If that snake is her honest choice, so be it. But I must know it with my own mind.

"Keep the candle in the window every night, Ham," he instructed. "Don't let it burn out in case Em'ly comes home. I've burned it there for so many years, and when she sees it she'll know she's welcome to her home and our hearts."

In the morning, Ham drove Daniel, Peggotty, and me to the London coach. Before we three boarded, Ham took me aside.

"There's no changing his mind, Davy. She's the center of his heart—always has been since she was orphaned by the sea. Try to keep in touch with him, Davy."

"I'll do what I can," was all I could promise.

Arriving in London that afternoon we got a room where Peggotty could stay while Barkis' estate was being finalized, then all went to dinner in the hotel restaurant. I asked Daniel about his plans, where he meant to go, but all he would answer was, "I'm going to look for Em'ly."

Folding his napkin and laying it beside his coffee cup, he rose and said it was time to leave. We walked with him to the hotel porch. He promised to keep in touch often to let us know where he was and how his search was going, but more than that he wouldn't say.

It was a warm, dusty evening with a ruby sunset. Daniel hugged Peggotty and me, then stepped off the porch and into the road. He turned, alone, at the corner of the shady street, into a glow of fading sunlight, and was gone.

CHAPTER 10

Blissful

I kept on loving Dora. Thinking of her was my refuge when everything was sad or in upset. I wasn't just crazy about her—I was drowning in love.

A week after Daniel left London, Mr. Spenlow told me his daughter was having a birthday and invited me to join them and some other friends for a picnic on Sunday. My excitement was boundless. I bought new clothes—boots too tight, a shirt too expensive. I rented a grey mare to ride, and at sunup Sunday I was in the flower stalls at Covent Garden buying a bouquet of roses and baby's breath for the Birthday Girl, tucking them into the silk band on my hat to keep them fresh for the gallop out to the country.

I found Dora sitting among the butterflies on a garden seat under a huge lilac bush—a lovely sight in a white bonnet and a dress of sky blue. Her dog Jip, a yappy little furball with slim patience for anyone but his mistress, and her friend Julia Mills were with her. My flowers pleased her, and she kept them at hand and sniffed them often, throwing direct and flirting glances at me over their tops. I was in paradise.

We all rode some miles into the countryside where a couple dozen Spenlow family members and friends had raised a brightly striped tent, tossed large quilts about on the grass, and set up nets and hoops for games. There was music and singing, food and champagne, play and dancing, and a bonfire. A perfect day— except that Dora didn't know my feelings. So three days later I told her. In grand phrases and with eloquent vows, I spoke of my loving as no one had loved before, of my wishing to perish if without her love in return, of my dreams for our marvelous future. She trembled. I knelt. She wept. I pleaded. She laughed. I spun her around until we were dizzy. She loved me. She loved me!

And so we were engaged. My happiness was complete. In its bright and quiet intensity, it formed a cushion to all my days, making holidays out of workdays, vacations out of weekends, and journeys of my every night's dreaming.

I loved Dora. Dora loved me. It was enough.

Peggotty and I returned from a walk through the markets to find Aunt Betsey Trotwood and the faithful Mr. Bick in the boardinghouse hallway. My aunt sat on one of a half-dozen trunks with her two birds in a cage and her tabby cat nestled into the sling her skirt formed between her knees. Mr. Bick stood bolt-upright, staring at my door.

"Aunt Betsey, Mr. Bick! Welcome!" I shouted. "Aunt, you remember Peggotty, don't you?"

Peggotty looked worried when she realized this was the aunt she'd last seen on the night I was born, the one who'd so upset my mother. Aunt Betsey gave her hand a firm shake and told her how sorry she was to hear about her recent loss.

We went inside, settled ourselves, and I waited to hear why they'd come so unexpect-

edly—and so fully packed. For a few minutes no one said anything. A curious and unusual process of hesitation appeared to be going on within my aunt.

"Trot," she finally began, "have you become self-reliant?"

"I think so, Aunt."

"And why do you suppose I'm sitting here on top of all my trunks, with my budgies and my cat and my dear companion Mr. Bick?"

I shook my head, unable to guess.

"Because it's all I have," she said. "I'm ruined. I have nothing but the cottage left." She said this not with despair or anger, but with confidence. "It's the fact, Trot. We've got to meet our bad times boldly and not let them frighten us."

I knew I would hear all of the story when she was ready to share it, but until then we needed to get everyone a place to stay. Peggotty was leaving in the morning for Yarmouth, but her room was so small that my aunt's trunks and birds and cat would have flowed into the hall. So I offered Aunt Betsey my bedroom and moved my things into the sitting room beside the sofa where I would sleep. I took Mr. Bick around the corner to another house with rooms to rent. The landlady apologized for the tininess of the available room, saying there was barely room to swing a cat. Mr. Bick assured her he didn't keep pets, and that the room was just delightful, thank you very much.

I left him staring out the window and went back around to my house. Aunt Betsey was pacing back and forth the length of my sitting-room, twisting the ruffled edges of her night-cap, when I went in. I poured some ale for both of us and we sat in the candlelight. We talked of Peggotty and of Barkis' death, of Em'ly's hasty leaving and Daniel's search, and finally of Dora and my lighthearted love.

"Lighthearted? More lightheaded!" cried my aunt. "Silly and impractical and selfish, like many young creatures."

Aunt Betsey calmed herself and said, "Earnestness and dedication and patience are better sought in lovers, and there is someone who offers you all of that. But I can tell your heart is set on Dora."

It was a few moments before she spoke again, this time quietly, almost too softly to be heard: "Ah, Trot, blind, blind, blind!"

I was locking the office door at Doctors' Commons the next afternoon when a carriage drew to a sharp stop at the curb not three feet from me. A graceful hand stretched out the window, followed by a face I never saw without feeling serene and happy in its presence.

"Agnes!" I shouted. "Of all people on earth, this is a surprise and a pleasure! Where are you going?"

She stepped out of the carriage, sending the driver away, and said she was on her way to my house to see my aunt. She'd gotten a typically odd and abrupt note from Aunt Betsey saying she'd fallen on difficult times and was leaving Dover. Agnes had come at once to London, but not alone for her father and Uriah Heep were along on business.

"I suppose they're partners now," I said. "Confound that evil man! Does he exert the same influence over your father?"

"Things are so much changed," Agnes said. "They live with us—Uriah and his mother. He sleeps in your old room. The worst part is that Uriah puts himself so much between Papa and me now that I can't watch over him as well as I could before." She slipped her arm through mine and I felt her tremble.

My aunt was delighted with the surprise visitor and the two women huddled immediately in quiet conversation. I fixed tea and joined them. We began to talk of my aunt's losses.

"I had some property," she said. "and made some good investments on the advice of your own father, Agnes. Then he seemed to change, and Uriah Heep entered, meddling in my account, so I no longer felt I could rely on wise counsel from the Wickfield firm. I made some bad decisions, and that's what happened. Lost it all—well, very close to all. And here I am at the kind mercy of my dear Trot."

"Aunt, you're welcome to everything I have," I said. "You and Mr. Bick and I are going to be a fine family again!"

We sat talking about our pleasant old Canterbury days for a couple of hours, then Agnes and I went for dinner at an inn close by. How

sweet it was to sit with her—how peaceful I always felt. I told her about Dora, and Agnes wished me every blessing and joy.

We walked back to her hotel and said goodnight. As I crossed the road and glanced back up at her window, a beggar crouched in the shadows called out to me:"Blind! Blind! Blind!"

I was out early the next day. My plan was to find an extra job or two during my apprenticeship that would add to the very small salary I received from Spenlow and Jorkin so that I could provide for my aunt and for Mr. Bick. I went first to see an old schoolmaster. He'd been writing a dictionary for all the years I'd known him and had often complained of having no assistant he could count on. I found his poor eyesight much more advanced than the number of alphabet letters completed, and we arrived at a work and pay schedule that suited us both.

My next visit was to Tommy Traddles' office. We'd talked before about work as a freelance reporter covering debates in the

Houses of Parliament. I wanted to do it and needed his advice. I took Mr. Bick with me because I thought there might be a chance of coming up with something useful that he could do there.

"How's your penmanship? Do you make letters that are clean and easily read?" Traddles asked Mr. Bick. "Do you think you could make copies of written papers, rewriting them on clean sheets of paper, exactly as the originals are written?"

I said I thought so, Traddles said he hoped so, and Mr. Bick said he'd certainly like to try it. He wanted to start at once, so Traddles got him set up at a corner desk with some contracts that needed to be copied for four partners.

Thereafter, Mr. Bick was up each day before dawn and off to Traddles' office. He worked fast and wrote clearly, and every week he brought a pay envelope to my aunt.

"No starving now!" he declared. "I'll provide for you with these." And he waved his ten inky fingers around in the air above his head, smiling his biggest smile.

After about a week of working all day at Doctors' Commons and then spending several hours either on the dictionary or scribbling furious notes of the heated discussions at Parliament, I went to visit Dora.

She came to the parlor door to greet me, and Jip shot past her skirt's hem, yapping and snapping at my pant's cuffs as if to warn away the worst robber. She scooped him up with a

quick tap to the nose, and I followed her into the garden. We sat in silence on a stone bench while I gazed with delight at her perky nose and pointy little chin.

"Dora," I blurted out without any preparation, "can you love a beggar?"

"How can you ask anything so silly?" she cried.

"Because, my dearest, that is just what I am," I said.

I put my arms around her and said that I loved her too much to keep her bound in an engagement with a man so poor as I, but that I would never recover if I lost her. I explained the drain on my finances and how I was working several ways to provide for all those who relied on me.

"And when we're married, we'll have to be practical. My aunt is handy with a needle and can show you how to sew," I said.

Dora made a noise halfway between a sob and a squeal.

"And it would help so much if you would read a little about cooking and keeping a household budget—"

This time it was a full-throated scream. Jip set to growling and barking and snapping at my leg. Dora's friend Julia came running from the house, clearly certain that warriors had broken through the trellises.

Dora would not be comforted and Julia led her away to her room. I sat in the garden, cursing myself for being a vicious beast, until Julia came back.

"Mr. Copperfield, Dora is not a strong person," Julia said, sadly. "She's made of light and air. She's been pampered all her life, and she's not going to take well to any change in that. The practical realities are entirely beyond her. She's had a terrific upset just now, but she'll be alright. If there's any hope of her making peace with household duties, I'll encourage her in it. But don't count on it."

I left in a very low mood and sat at the pub for an hour trying to cheer myself up. Well! I loved her and there was no changing that. And I would go on loving her entirely, and working harder than ever. That night I fell asleep wishing life were more peaceful and Dora were more like Agnes.

I arrived at Doctors' Commons one morning several weeks later to find a small crowd in the street outside our offices. The central door stood open and I could see all the clerks inside.

"It's the worst calamity," said Tiffy, the office manager. "Mr. Spenlow's dead! I found him this morning. The doctor says it must have been his heart. Awful!"

There was a terrible vacancy in Mr. Spenlow's office, where his desk and chair seemed to wait for him, and the handwriting on his tablet was like a ghost. I expected him to come in at any moment, not to be gone from here for all time.

There was a flurry of unanticipated activity to be handled that day, clients to be contacted, appointments to be changed. When I left the Commons I took a coach out to the country, to Norwood, to comfort Dora.

Julia Mills met me at the gate and said that Dora was much too upset to see anyone, even me. "She can only cry and cry," she said. "She

needs to sleep. This has been too much of a shock for someone as delicate as Dora. I'll tell her you came by and I'm sure she'll be in touch with you soon, Mr. Copperfield."

There was no reaching my grieving love, so I returned to London. And no word came from her the rest of the week. Mr. Jorkins found that Mr. Spenlow was a better preacher than a practicer—he had made no will, had overspent his personal budget, and was all but penniless.

At the start of the next week, a letter came for me from Julia. She explained that Dora had at last recovered herself a bit and that Mr. Spenlow's two sisters had come to take her home with them to Putney. The house was to be closed and sold. Dora, she wrote, would surely write me as soon as she was able.

I felt as if I had been living in a palace of playing cards, and that a large puff of wind had blown it all to the ground.

CHAPTER 11

Wickfield and Heep

My aunt asked me to go to Dover to
look after the rental of her home. I
think she knew if I got to Dover I'd go
all the way to Canterbury and there see Agnes—
a certain cure for worry and depression.

I found everything in good condition at the
cottage, settled the few details with her new ten-
ant, and in the morning walked to Canterbury. It
was the early edge of winter and a fresh, cold
wind was sweeping downland. Canterbury was
hardly changed from the days of my schooling
there. The same shops with the same people.

Well, not everyone was the same! There
was a new employee at the offices of Wick-

field and Heep—none other than Mr. Micawber, now serving as Uriah's confidential clerk. He and I were both surprised when I walked into the office that used to be Heep's.

"Something turned up!" Micawber exclaimed, shaking my hand like a pump handle. "I never doubted it would, did I?"

"How do you like the law?" I asked.

"Well, it's not the place for a man with any imagination," he sighed. "So many details weigh down the soul. Still, it's good work."

I asked where he and the family were living, and he said they were renting the house that Uriah and his mother had vacated. "It's very humble," he said with a wink.

"And how is Uriah treating you?"

"Davy, beggars can't be choosers, you know. But I've found Heep to be very generous with me in my misfortunes, and when I've needed a little extra cash a time or two, he's given it to me. I have nothing ill to say of him."

Although I sensed some discomfort in Mr. Micawber's manner, it wasn't my place to prod him for more information. It seemed there was some barrier now between us that kept away our old friendliness.

Agnes was sitting by the fire in the parlor, her pen gliding smoothly over a tablet on her lap. The bright change in her face when she saw me at the door was a huge boost to my low spirits.

"I've missed you so much, Agnes," I said when we were seated. "Seeing you here in these rooms where we spent so much time before reminds me how naturally I used to come to you for advice and support—and how much I feel the lack of it. Here in this room with you, I'm home, in peace and happiness, like a very tired traveler about to get some rest."

"Trotwood, I shouldn't be the source of advice and reliance for you," Agnes replied with a pleasant smile. "That you must get from Dora."

"In any other world, I'd agree, Agnes," I said. "But Dora is rather difficult to rely upon. She's timid and easily frightened."

I told Agnes all that had happened—the engagement, my declaration of poverty, Mr. Spenlow's death, and Dora's move to Putney in the care of her aunts. "What do I do now that I've made a mess of it all?"

She suggested I write the two aunts and ask to visit them, and I set my mind to write and mail the letter that afternoon.

"And on the subject of couples, Agnes," I said, "promise me you won't marry Heep!"

She looked at me as if I'd gone crazy. "Marry him?" she questioned. "I despise him."

"But don't let him use your father's welfare to win you," I pleaded.

"Trot!" she said firmly. "There'll be no further partnerships between Wickfield and Heep."

The winter stretched ahead and behind in equal measure. I'd come back from Canterbury and dug myself into my many jobs. One bitter-cold evening, I walked home along St. Martin's Lane. The snow lay so thick that the noise of wheels and people's footsteps were as hushed as if the streets had been covered knee-deep with feathers.

I stopped to let a carriage pass before I crossed the street and a woman stepped up

beside me. I briefly saw her face before she pulled her scarf over her hair, turned in the other direction, and was gone. I knew the face—from somewhere, some time. Where?

On the church steps a man was stooping over and straightening up, shifting the weight of some large sack to his shoulder. At the very moment I recognized Peggotty's brother Daniel, I knew the woman had been Martha Endell of Yarmouth, to whom Em'ly had given money that night in Peggotty's kitchen.

"Davy!" Daniel's shout was muffled in floating snow. We clasped hands and stood for several seconds, too surprised to talk. "I was coming to see you in the morning," he said.

There was a coffeehouse at the corner with a blazing fire and lots of empty tables so we settled ourselves there to warm away the frozen night. I studied Daniel as he shed several wet layers of clothing. His hair was long and ragged, greyer than before. Sun and wind had darkened his skin and deepened the lines around his eyes and mouth. But strong!—he looked stronger than I'd ever seen him.

He told me of his journey across the English Channel to France, traveling there by foot and horsecart. In every town he would tell his story and ask if Em'ly'd been seen—he told it so much it began to spread on its own, sometimes getting to the next town before he did. People took him in, fed him, gave him a bed every place he went. But there was no news of Em'ly until one man said he'd seen the servant with a man and a woman and heard the two men speak of going to a village in the Swiss mountains.

"I went there direct, Davy. But I was too late," Daniel explained. Em'ly had been and gone off to a place in Germany near the Upper Rhine. Daniel was bound there in the morning.

We went into the snowy night and Daniel crossed the road, turning back once to wave. Everything seemed, in my imagination, to be hushed in reverence for him as he took up again his lonely journey in the snow.

CHAPTER 12

My Dora, Again

At last, an answer came from Dora's two old aunts. I was welcome to visit them and discuss the proposed courtship in person. They specified a day and time, and told me I could bring along a trusted friend. As soon as I accepted their invitation and arranged for Tommy Traddles to accompany me there, I fell into serious nervous agitation.

When the maid opened the door, I had a mild sensation of being on view. We went across a hall into a quiet drawing-room. The glass doors at back opened onto a garden. An old-fashioned mantel clock ticked steadily—in a rhythm that didn't match my pounding heart. It seemed to tick a thousand times before the brittle, little, black-gowned sisters entered the room.

"Do be seated," said one of them.

The sisters were birdlike, with bright and darting eyes and sudden mannerisms. They seemed to ruffle and adjust themselves, pertly and repeatedly, like canaries. Clarissa and Lavinia, as they called one another, were dressed alike, although the younger one wore her black dress with a perkier air—perhaps there was a little more frill to the sleeve or an extra bow. They both had excellent posture, formal and composed. One sister, the younger one, had my letter in her hand. The other kept her arms crossed over her breast and every few moments she seemed to tap out some unshared music on her upper arms.

"Mr. Copperfield?" said the sister with the letter.

"My sister Lavinia," said the younger woman, "will tell you what we believe will promote the greatest happiness of all parties concerned."

"Thank you, Clarissa," said the other.

Each of the sisters leaned a bit forward to speak, shook her head after speaking, and straightened up in silence.

"We have no reason," said Miss Lavinia, "to believe you are anything but an honorable young man. And we believe you care for our niece."

Given to a bad case of excess at just that moment, I exclaimed that nobody had ever loved anybody as I loved Dora. Traddles murmured in solid agreement.

"We understand that you believe what you say, but we need to see for ourselves," Miss Lavinia continued. "And so we agree to your request to visit Dora here—only here. Can you abide by that, Mr. Copperfield?"

I bound myself immediately to the required promise.

The sisters laid out a schedule of visits— Sunday dinner at three o'clock and tea at half-past six two evenings a week—and asked me to invite my aunt to visit them. Then they stood, said good-bye to Traddles and to me, and left us to the care of the maid who showed us out.

Now my full days were overflowing. Work in civil law, dictionary writing, Parliament reporting, *and* courting! I lived for my times at Putney.

In all the excited bliss of this courtship there was one troublesome point for me. I saw the Spenlows, and indeed even Aunt Betsey, treating Dora like a child—no, more like a pet. She was pampered and spoiled, treated much the way she treated Jip. Dora didn't seem to mind, though.

I was amazed when Dora asked me to give her a cookbook and to show her how to keep the household accounts, according to my earlier suggestion. Within the week, however, the cookbook had made my love's head ache and when the figures wouldn't add up they made her cry, so all was put aside and life went on as before. Even I wondered occasionally if I'd slipped into the general fault of treating her like a pleasant child.

***

Mr. Wickfield had business in London and Agnes traveled with him from Canterbury for a two-week stay. I arranged with Miss Lavinia to bring Agnes to tea so she could meet Dora.

I was proud and nervous—proud of my beautiful Dora and worried sick that Agnes

wouldn't like her. But the gentle look on Agnes' face shook all of my fears aside, and the two young women became instant friends. In fact, when we finally departed for town, Agnes had only good things to say of Dora, and I basked in the glow of her words like settling into warm sunlight.

Weeks, months, seasons passed—flew by so quickly that they felt like no more than a summer day and a winter evening. I left Doctors' Commons and the civil law and took a job with the *London Morning Chronicle* as a reporter; I also began to write fiction. When my first piece, written and submitted in secret, was published in a popular magazine, I set to writing regularly and built a reputation among readers.

By my twenty-first birthday, my income had risen comfortably. The Spenlow sisters gave their happy consent, and Dora and I prepared to marry.

What a bustle of activity it was for everyone in our small families. Miss Lavinia took on the wardrobe task. Miss Clarissa and Aunt Betsey scoured London for furniture. Peggotty set to cleaning and recleaning, polishing and repolishing every inch of our new cottage. Agnes and Sophy, Traddles' fiancée, outfitted themselves as bridesmaids, and Mr. Bick practiced time and again his conducting my precious Dora down the church aisle and onto my waiting arm.

The groom, however, remained in a fog! I felt misty and unsettled, as if I'd gotten up very early in the morning a week or two ago and hadn't been to bed since. Nothing was real to the touch. It all swirled around me, like a dream I could see but not take part in. A happy, flustered, hurried dream!

Then suddenly it was the wedding day. Senses were exaggerated: smells were stronger, colors brighter, sounds closer to my ears.

Dora came into the church with Mr. Bick— lovely she was, grinning he was. Miss Lavinia was the first to sob. Aunt Betsey tried her best to be firm, but tears rolled down her face.

Dora shook terribly at my side and made her wedding responses in tiny whispers, then collapsed in a massive cry for her dead father when we'd left the church. There was a wedding breakfast with tables full of food and champagne, and I made a toast to my bride and one to my dear family and friends.

The celebrating drew to a close in the late afternoon. Traddles had hired a carriage with a white horse and decorated it with flowers

and bows, and we rode away to the music of cheers and good wishes.

"Are you happy now, you foolish boy?" asked Dora, snuggling close beside me in the carriage. "Are you sure you don't regret this?"

I kissed her nose and told her I was sure.

We settled into our married life. All of the romance and yearning of our engagement were put aside in the daily presence of one another.

We were so young and so unprepared to keep house, but we got used to it. We hired a housekeeper who did a passable job—but Dora took no part in managing the daily chores. I spent long hours at my writing and my dear wife sat beside me petting Jip and drawing pictures of flowers. Home was not as I might have wanted, but it was home nonetheless.

CHAPTER 13

Word and Hope

A bout a year after my wedding to Dora, I passed in front of Mrs. Steerforth's house. As I walked by her front step, I heard a voice call out my name.

It was Rosa Dartle, young James' hammer target. She stepped through the door onto the porch, colorless, thin, and full of superiority. Our meeting was not to be cordial.

"Has the girl been found?" she asked.

I said she had not.

"She has run away." She looked intently at my face, her lips working from side to side.

"Run away?" I repeated.

"From him," she said, with a cold laugh. "If she hasn't been found by now, perhaps she's already dead!"

Her steady gaze was cruel.

"Do you want the details?" she asked. She stepped back into the hallway and I heard her call for Littimer, who joined her on the porch a moment later. He bowed in my direction.

"Tell him what you have told me," she instructed.

He had no reluctance to share his story. He and Steerforth had been in Europe with Em'ly. Steerforth and Em'ly had gotten along wonderfully, Em'ly proving quite ready and able to learn new languages and new manners, to adopt new and stylish ways of dressing and wearing her hair.

"She was admired wherever we went," he said.

But she was often in low spirits, unhappy and homesick. After a while that bothered Steerforth. It made him restless. And the more restless he got, the more unhappy she got, and things worsened.

"At last," Littimer explained, "after there'd been another nasty battle, Mr. James left. He told me to break to her the news that he would not be back, and he suggested that she would do well to marry a respectable person, like myself."

When Littimer told Em'ly that Steerforth was gone for good, she flew to pieces. He said she had to be held by force and kept from sharp objects and the sea, for fear that she would harm herself.

Littimer had locked her up in a room of the villa but during the night she broke the window and escaped, not to be seen again.

I felt both terror for Em'ly, now truly alone in the world, and joy that she was free.

There was nothing else to say, and I left quickly. By the time I reached our cottage, I was determined to find Daniel and tell him the news, such as it was. The next evening I went into the heart of London. Since the night of the big snow, so long ago, when he'd been bound for Germany, I'd seen Daniel several times. Although he wandered from place to place, continent to island, in his sad quest, he was most often in London. I would see him in the dead of night passing along streets, searching among the few who huddled in doorways or slept on benches. I knew he kept a room over the candle shop in Hungerford Market, whether at home or away, and I went there.

He was at home, happy to see a friendly face.

"Don't expect much, but I have some news of Em'ly," I said as I sat down. "I don't know where she is, but she is not with him."

I told him Littimer's story, sparing no details. Then we sat silently for several minutes.

"What do you think, Davy? Is she alive?" he asked.

"I think she is," I answered. He agreed.

"Daniel, if she makes her way to London, and what better place to come and hide herself among thousands," I said, "I think there's someone here who's likely to discover her."

I asked if he remembered Martha Endell from Yarmouth. He said that he had seen her some of the nights when he'd gone searching London's boat docks and on the streets.

I told him I had seen her too and I thought we should try to find her and ask about Em'ly.

"I may know where to look for her, Davy," Daniel said. "It's dark enough to go now."

For an hour we went up and down streets in the big and dirty city. We were not far from Blackfriars Bridge when Daniel turned his head and pointed to a female figure moving along the opposite side of the street.

"Let's follow a bit and see where she goes," I whispered.

We stayed at a distance, keeping her in sight as we weaved in and out of groups of people. She turned down an empty street heading for the river. At the water's edge she stopped and moved slowly along it, looking intently at the black current.

"Martha!" my shout startled her.

"Martha, it's Em'ly's Uncle Daniel and David Copperfield," I said. Slowly she came in our direction. "We need your help—Em'ly needs your help."

She heard our story and asked what possible good she could be in finding Em'ly. "It's likely that she'll make her own way back to London, if she's at all able to travel," I said. "If you see her, shelter her, and get word to us."

I wrote our addresses on a slip of paper that she tucked into her thin coat. We followed her a short distance until we reached the busy streets. Then Daniel and I went home, parting with a prayer for the success of this fresh effort.

In the months after Daniel and I spoke with Martha on the riverbank, we heard nothing from or about Em'ly, and I began to give up hope of finding her. Daniel stayed certain that she was alive and would be found, and he kept up the search.

He was used to visiting Dora and me when he was in London and one evening he arrived in some excitement. He'd met with Martha the night before and she asked him not to leave the city for any reason. She wouldn't say why or when he'd see her again, and she insisted he give her his promise.

Almost two weeks later I was alone in our garden when I saw a small, cloaked figure across the road motioning to me. Martha!

"Can you come with me?" she whispered. "Can you come now?"

Martha said she had already left a note for Daniel, so I flagged an empty coach and told the driver to take us quickly to Golden Square, according to Martha's instructions.

We got out in front of a long row of large apartment buildings, and I followed Martha up

the central stairway of the third house from the corner, a passageway swarming with renters. We ran to the top story of the house and Martha stopped dead in her tracks on the last step.

"Someone's just gone into my room!" she hissed back at me. "Someone I don't know."

Martha led me through a small door with no latch. We could hear voices, but saw nothing.

"—don't care about her. It's you I've come to see," a woman was saying.

"Me? But I don't know you," was the soft reply. Em'ly—it was Em'ly's voice!

"I'm here to get a look at you," the first woman said. A shiver ran through me as I recognized the snappish sound—Rosa Dartle. There was unrelenting hatred in her tone.

"I wanted to see the sorceress who took James Steerforth to his doom," she exclaimed. "So here she is, and what an ugly and pathetic creature! You must have bewitched him for him to consider you worth a moment of his time."

"Please don't say such things of me," Em'ly begged.

"Have you thought," cried Rosa, "of the harm you have done to the family?"

"I think of nothing else but my poor uncle and of Ham and the pain I've—"

"What?" came the strangled screech. "Such vanity for an earthworm! You think I care about *your* family? I'm talking about *his* family, *his* home—where I live."

"No!" shouted Em'ly. "I believed him, trusted and loved him."

"*You* loved him? *You*? Disgusting!" Rosa shrieked. Then a shrill, joyless laugh followed. It was quiet in the room for several seconds and when she spoke again Rosa's voice was low and dripped with acid: "I can't breathe in the same air as you. If you are still here tomorrow, your true character will be shouted in all four directions. Go away or die!"

We heard Martha's door open, and at the same moment I heard a sturdy tread on the steps. I stepped out into the hall and saw Rosa push past a small gathering of people at the top of the stairs. Daniel's head rose over the landing and he came up at a run, not pausing before he rushed into the room with the open door.

"Uncle!"

There was a loud sob and we reached Martha's door just as Daniel caught the fainting Em'ly in his arms.

"My dream's come true, Davy!" he shouted over the crowd. "I knew it would!"

Daniel was at our kitchen door early the next morning. He came inside and Aunt Betsey poured us all a cup of tea.

"Trot's been telling me about the miracle," she said to him. "How did Em'ly get back?"

It was several pots of tea and a basket of biscuits later when the story was all told. Em'ly had escaped from Littimer at night, frightened and confused and lost. Believing Daniel's old boat-house was moored close by, she went running along the sea-beach to find it. She cut her arms and feet as she ran and fell on the sharp stones of the beach, and finally exhausted herself so she couldn't get up the last time she fell. It was daylight, cold and gusty, when she woke. She was covered by an old coat and there was a woman sitting beside her. She took Em'ly back to her cottage. Em'ly was sick with fever for a week, but when the fever broke she slept peacefully for two days. She came to her senses on a beautiful Sunday morning, thinking she was home in Yarmouth, and her heart broke fresh when she realized she was nowhere close to anything familiar. When she got strong again, the woman and her brother put her aboard a small trading ship going to Leghorn, Switzerland, and then to France. She had taken a job as a maid for traveling women at an inn, and one day she thought she saw Steerforth. That was enough of a fright to set her off for England and she set ashore at Dover.

"Em'ly went to London, without a penny," Daniel said, and my aunt clucked and shook her head for the fiftieth time. "There aren't many choices for a poor young woman in the city, and Martha Endell knew just where to keep an eye out. I'll owe her a debt of gratitude all my life."

"Are you taking Em'ly back to Yarmouth?" I asked.

"No home for her there anymore," Daniel sighed. "Nor here either, I'm sure. There are great countries far from these shores, and our future lies in one of them. I've been thinking of Australia. No one there will know what she's been through. A ship leaves in eight weeks and we'll be leaving on it."

Daniel had to take the news of the glad return to Peggotty and to Ham in Yarmouth, and he wanted company for the trip. I agreed to go.

The ride to the seaside village was quickened by our high spirits. We went at once to Peggotty's house where delight at the news set her to jumping and singing. Ham came in toward the end of the story and took the knowledge that Em'ly was safe at last with a calm thanksgiving. Something about the way he looked at me when we all said good night suggested there were things left unspoken and I went looking for him at the boatyard the next morning.

"Davy, have you seen her?" he asked when we'd left the dock.

"Only unconscious in Daniel's arms," I answered. "It might be too painful for her right now to see anyone but Daniel. But if there's a message you want to send, I'll find a way to get it to her, Ham."

"I loved her, Davy. You know that." He said this so earnestly my heart ached for the hurt that years had not quelled. "But she's had enough grief to bear and she needs no more guilt heaped on that. Can you find a way to let her think I'm no longer mourning for her and that I'm not tired of life?"

I said I'd try to set her heart at peace but, walking back to meet Peggotty and Daniel, I wondered how I could convince her of something I didn't believe.

CHAPTER 14

Money Found,
People Lost

A letter came to me from Mr. Micawber in Canterbury. My old friend loved to write and fancied that he did it well. In fact, he made such a muddle of his meaning that two or three readings were needed to crack the rambling code. After reading his letter, all I knew for certain was that he was coming to London in two days and wanted me to meet him. Mr. Micawber added a note that he'd asked Tommy Traddles to meet him, too.

On Saturday we met at the designated spot and exchanged greetings. He took the arms that Traddles and I offered and the three of us walked off in the direction of the carriage stop.

On the ride to my house near Highgate, I asked about Agnes and Mr. Wickfield.

"Miss Wickfield," said Micawber, blushing a bit, "is the only starry spot in a miserable household. She is love and truth and goodness!"

Mr. Micawber seemed so low-spirited and weakened that no one ventured any conversation in the carriage. Only when my aunt held him in light conversation later that evening did he rouse himself to share his despair.

"Villainy is the trouble!" he nearly shouted. "And deception, and fraud, and conspiracy. The name at the center is Heep!"

The floodgates opened and descriptions of Heep poured out: detestable serpent, immoral hypocrite, perjurer, rascal, doomed traitor, liar and cheat. With each one, Micawber became more breathless and red-faced. I thought he might explode on the spot.

At length, he ran out of steam.

"I have to go," he said more quietly. "But I ask that all of you come to Canterbury one

week from today. And there you'll see an end
to evil."

Nothing would have kept the four of us
from Canterbury that next Saturday. We went
on Friday night and met Micawber for breakfast at a hotel in the center of town.

Our host was too excited to eat. "I trust
you'll soon see an eruption, friends," he told
us. He asked us to give him a five-minute start
and then to come to the office of Wickfield
and Heep and ask to see Agnes. He had nothing else to say. With a waist-deep bow, he was
off down the street. Exactly five minutes later,
we stepped into the street and went three
doors down to witness an explosion.

Micawber was seated at the reception desk
in the first office. He greeted us all as if we'd
not just been together and asked what brought
us to Canterbury. I said we'd come to see
Agnes and was she in?

He led us to the dining-room and threw
open the doors.

219

"Miss Betsey Trotwood, Mr. David Copperfield, Mr. Thomas Traddles, and Mr. Bick!" he said in a booming voice that thoroughly startled the man seated at the dining table reading the morning news—Heep.

Uriah jumped to his feet in astonishment, for the briefest moment frowning so badly his small red eyes were nearly closed. In a heartbeat this look was replaced with a sickly, humble smile and posture.

"An unexpected—undeserved—pleasure!" he cried. "Such a joy to have all friends gathered 'round at once. Micawber, make sure Agnes and Mother know who's come to see us. They'll be so glad."

"Not too busy for us, Heep?" asked Traddles.

"Not at all," Heep answered. "Not so busy as I'd wish to be. Lawyers, sharks, and leeches are not easily satisfied, you know!"

Agnes came in, not as serene but every bit as lovely as always. I saw Uriah watch her while she greeted us, and I shivered a bit.

"You can go, Micawber," Uriah said, dismissing his clerk with a wave of his bony hand. Micawber stood still at the door, looking directly at his employer.

"Are you deaf?" Uriah croaked at his clerk. "Didn't you hear me tell you to leave?"

"I heard you," Micawber said.

"Then why are you still here?"

"Because I choose to be here!" Micawber replied in a burst.

Uriah's cheeks lost color and a sickly paleness, barely tinged with his usual red glow, spread over them.

"You're a worthless man, as all the world knows," he shot at Micawber, "and one of these days you'll force me to fire you." With a struggle to appear pleasant before his guests, he half-smiled and said quietly, "Now go along and we'll talk later."

With a sudden anger that startled us all, Micawber shouted, "If there's a scoundrel on earth with whom I've already talked too much, that scoundrel's name is HEEP!"

Uriah fell back as if he'd been struck, and looked around at each of us with a dark and wicked expression.

"Oh, I see! We've a conspiracy here. You've all met by appointment. Is this your doing, Copperfield?" He'd broken into a clammy sweat on his face and a skinny hand wiped at his forehead. "Agnes, if you love your father, don't join this gang. I'll ruin him if you do."

Traddles spoke up then: "That will not be, Mr. Heep. I'm Mr. Wickfield's friend and his protector."

"The old man has drunk himself into stupidity," Uriah charged, turning uglier than before, "and you've got his trust from him by fraud!"

"Something has been got by fraud, I know," Traddles said quietly, "and you know it, too, Mr. Heep."

In an instant, the mask of humility that Heep had worn for so long was gone, and the open face of malice took its place.

Micawber stepped into the center of the room and said, "I came to work for a firm doing business as Wickfield and Heep, but Heep alone is the force here. Heep alone is the forger and the cheat!"

"These are my charges against you, Mr. Heep," Micawber continued, "and I have proof for every one: when Mr. Wickfield was least able to conduct business, you got his signature

223

on papers that gave you access to his money; you wrote phony payments and kept the proceeds; you forged his name to documents; and you kept false books of account, stealing from him and your clients at every opportunity."

Uriah cast a glance at the iron safe in the corner of the room. He went to it and threw the doors open with a huge clank. It was empty.

"Where are the books?" he cried, making a frightful face. "Some thief has stolen them!"

"I have them," Traddles told him. "They're not your concern any longer. Your concern now and for as long as it takes is repayment of every penny you have stolen. The Wickfields and all of your clients will have their property restored."

At that a blur of dark blue taffeta and ostrich feathers flew at Heep's neck.

"Thieving snake!" Aunt Betsey screamed as she yanked at his collar with both gloved hands. "You took everything I had and thought nothing of it! I could choke the evil wind from you right here!"

I wrapped my arms around her waist and pulled her back from Heep. "You'll get everything back, Aunt. We'll see to it," I said.

Uriah at last gave up and slipped into the chair behind his desk. Traddles told him calmly that he would have no trouble calling the police and securing a proper room for him at

Maidstone Jail if there was any hesitancy to sign a promise of repayment. Defeat sat heavily on Uriah's scrawny shoulders as the rest of us left him with Traddles.

In the hallway I found Mr. Bick giving Mr. Micawber a hearty hug. Agnes had gone to see to her father's needs and Aunt Betsey stood straightening her feathered bonnet at the mirror.

"Well, I'm not sorry I'll be looking for other work," Mr. Micawber announced. "Something's sure to turn up!"

"I wonder, Mr. Micawber, if you've ever considered living abroad," said my aunt.

"A dream of my youth, madam!" Micawber answered.

"I know of a fine family leaving in several weeks for Australia. It's a prime place for a man who conducts himself honestly and works hard. This might be just the time then for you and your family to make the move," Aunt Betsey offered.

"Well, it's a capital idea and it's a capital problem, Miss Trotwood. There's no money to finance such a dream."

"If it's only money, Mr. Micawber, that can be found. Come see me in London next week and we'll make some arrangements," she said.

⚜

In the weeks following Heep's destruction, my precious Dora grew weaker. She never ran and seldom walked more than a few slow steps. She looked wonderful and was in good spirits, but her legs grew lifeless. I carried her up and down stairs each day. After a time, our doctor stopped holding out hope for a recovery. Aunt Betsey and I sat for hours with her.

"Ah, Davy, she said one day, "I don't think I've been a very good wife."

Tears came to my eyes. "Every bit as good a wife as I have been a husband," I told her. "We've been very happy, and I would not have changed a single thing."

"I want to see Agnes," Dora said. "Do you think she would come, even with her father needing care?"

Of course, Agnes came the day the request reached her. She joined Aunt Betsey and me at Dora's bedside, and sat with us morning to night. On the third evening of Agnes' visit, after my Aunt had gone to her room, Dora asked me to kiss her and to leave her alone with Agnes so they could talk. I sat on the bed and gathered her into my arms—how tiny she was!

"You could not have loved me any better, Davy," she said. "I've been so happy."

I carried Jip, by now as frail as his mistress, downstairs with me and he waddled to his blanket. Stretching out at my feet as if to sleep, he gave a little cry. I looked up at Agnes in the doorway, and saw in her face that Dora was dead.

The days until the funeral were a blur. I know that friends called to comfort me, and neighbors brought flowers and food. Mr. Bick was my best companion; he sat and said nothing and expected nothing from me. Nothing was all I had to give.

I think it was Agnes who suggested I take a trip abroad, to put space between me and the sorrowful places of London, and I agreed to go when the final matters of Heep's thievery were settled and when everyone bound for Australia had left.

At Traddles' request, Aunt Betsey and I went to Mr. Micawber's house in Canterbury to hear the results of the Heep investigations. And it was truly good news for my aunt. A full accounting of the books had located all of her missing funds. She had thought Mr. Wickfield had mismanaged that money and she covered up his error by saying she had invested poorly and lost it all herself. In fact, Heep had embezzled the fortune. Aunt Betsey's money and all of the money Heep had stolen from Mr. Wickfield's business had not been spent, but merely squirreled away for future need. True to her own style, Aunt Betsey asked Traddles to set aside a portion of the money for the Micawbers' traveling costs so they could emigrate to Australia and start over.

"And what has become of the devious Heep?" my aunt asked.

"He and his mother are gone," Traddles answered. "They took a night coach to London and that's all I know."

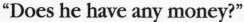
"Does he have any money?"

"I'm sure he pocketed a lot, one way or another," Traddles said. "But I don't think having money will ever keep him out of the Devil's company. His life's course is set for nothing good."

Little more than a week remained until the ship would leave England for Australia. Peggotty had come to London to spend the last days with Daniel and Em'ly. The Micawbers were in a flurry of preparation. And Ham's request that I set Em'ly's heart to rest was on my mind. I sent a letter to her through Daniel, telling her of Ham's forgiveness and his love. Daniel came to see me the same afternoon.

"Your letter has done her so much good!" He was delighted with the effect of Ham's forgiving her. "She's written this reply to Ham and asks that you send it on to him."

"There's time before your ship sails for me to go to Yarmouth and see to its delivery," I told him. "I'm in a restless mood these days and better off in motion. I'll go this evening on the late mail coach."

I set out for Yarmouth that night, anxious to put the precious document in Ham's hands, anxious for his life to begin anew.

But I didn't arrive in time. There were dreadful storms at sea off the coast and several

ships had broken apart. Their passengers and crews were dead. One ship bound for London from Portugal had come close to crashing into the docks at Yarmouth and a local sailor had died trying to rescue men who clung to its sinking mast.

When my carriage reached Yarmouth, I found the beach crowded with sailors, ship-builders, and townspeople. There was deafening storm noise. One ship's mast had broken off short above the schooner's deck. It lay over the side tangled in sailcloth and rigging. Men on board hacked with axes at the mast that was hammering the boat. A huge swell swept over the deck and carried men and debris into the sea. The ship righted and still four men clung to the mast. The ship was even closer to the shore, but the might of wind and water made reaching it impossible. Again the waves reached up and sucked them down, and again the ship came back—with only two men left.

There was commotion to my left—a man was being wrapped in roping by a group of sailors who were setting themselves to secure the ropes to shore while he tried the seas in a hopeless rescue attempt. It was Ham!

He bobbed in the swell for a minute or two. Only one man still clung to the mast as if hung there by fishing line. The ship's bell clanged a mournful tone and in that instant I had a sickening sensation of remembrance for a once-dear friend.

I saw Ham's face and shoulders rise in the surf. He was bleeding but motioning for more rope. He rose and sank, made progress toward the wreck, was thrown back toward the shore, and rose again. He was almost to his destination, then all was gone, ship, mast, sail, and men.

Pieces of the wreckage hit the shore with every thunderous wave, several bodies among them. Ham's washed up quite close to where I stood shaking in chill and fear. Three of us carried him to a battered shelter and had just covered his beaten face when a bargeman I knew came looking for me.

"Mister Davy, we've another out here you'll want to see, but we don't know about layin' him there by Ham," he said.

I followed him out on the side porch to where a body lay—the body of the last man on ship, my friend James Steerforth.

Perhaps for the exhaustion, or the terror, or the agonizing compounding of losses—I slumped to the floor in shuddering sobs and stayed there who knows how long.

My sleep that night was deep, though far from peaceful. Dora and Ham and Steerforth all flowed and bumped through my dreams. How very much I needed to face these losses of mine and give myself to the emotions that stirred like a tempest just below the surface of my control.

CHAPTER 15

Many Go and One Returns

Once I'd waved farewell to the deck full of travelers bound for Australia, everything I had to do in England was done. I packed and left for Europe. I'd thought the worst of all my sorrow was behind me but I was wrong. It only began when I left home. Without business or friends, I had only myself and all the losses and all the memories and all the canceled dreams for company. Desolation came on me slowly until its weight was crippling.

I'd been gone about nine months when a packet of letters caught up with me in Switzerland. One was from Agnes. I read it again and again. She didn't scold me for my wander-

237

ing absence—only wrote to encourage my
healing, saying she knew I would turn the hurt
to strength. And she urged me to begin writing again.

Write! Of course. Maybe writing could lift
the grey fog of despair. I crafted one and then
another novel, the characters peopling my life
and keeping me good company. And again I
traveled, this time with my eyes more open to
the sights. My health improved; in fact, I got
so much good air and exercise that I was in
better shape than I had ever been. The manu-
scripts I sent to Traddles were published and
well received, and I was sometimes even recognized. I began to come back to life.

I'd been gone about three years when the
need for England grew too strong to fight and
I turned toward home. My greatest longing
was for Agnes—the gentleness, the warmth,
the peace.

Aunt Betsey and Agnes both knew I was coming home but they thought that it would be close to Christmas. I planned to surprise them a few weeks before that.

On my first full day on London soil I took a coach to Dover and burst into my aunt's old parlor in the midst of afternoon tea. Aunt Betsey, Mr. Bick, and Peggotty, who was now their housekeeper, shot to their feet in a heartbeat and we all danced in a circle, laughing and shouting. We spent the evening catching up. I told them of the places and the sights I'd seen. They talked of Traddles' wedding to the lovely Sophy, and brought out the letters that had come from Australia. We marveled over Mr. Micawber's good fortune in the unsettled countryside. We took no surprise at Daniel's prosperity in farming and cattle-raising, and all were glad to know Em'ly was happy teaching a roomful of children.

When the others had gone to bed, Aunt Betsey and I sat with glasses of warm ale, listening to the frozen tree limbs tap against the cottage roof and staring at the fire.

"When are you going to Canterbury, Trot?" my aunt asked.

"I'll get a horse and ride over tomorrow morning," I said, "unless you'd like to go and then we'll get a carriage."

"Not this time. You go on ahead, without these old bones slowing you down. Go see Agnes."

I studied her beloved old profile as she watched the flames and was reminded of her once saying, "Blind, blind, blind." Now, too late, I understood her.

"Has she any —" I started, and stopped.

"What, Trot? Any what?"

"Is there any special person, any love in her life?"

"Oh, she could have been married twenty times, but I suspect she loves someone very special." Aunt Betsey finished her ale and stood up.

"A prosperous someone?" I asked.

"Trot, I don't know. She's confided nothing in me and I shouldn't have said this much. Blame it on an old woman's mutterings. Goodnight and welcome home."

I rode to Canterbury in the morning, filled to the brim with the memories of my schooldays passed in that town. Every hill and turn was precious.

The housekeeper who answered the door didn't know me and she told me to wait in the drawing-room. Nothing had been changed. The same books, the desk where I'd done my homework with Agnes' help, the emerald-green glass shade on the same brass lamp. Happy times rose like smoke around me.

Agnes flew through the little door in the paneled wall and I spun to catch her in a huge hug. Beautiful, the face that smiled so widely at me. We both talked at once, then both stopped, then laughed and started again. There was no end to our delight!

We sat together into the afternoon, talking and laughing, sometimes crying over the losses and the sorrows. And more than once I tried to tell her what her constant caring had meant to me during my time away, and for all the time I'd known her. I watched her closely as I spoke to see if there was any glimmer of interest beyond the dearest friendship that we shared. But I detected none. On my ride home I cursed myself for letting the ripe moment pass away years earlier.

I moved back into Aunt Betsey's cottage in Dover with Mr. Bick and Peggotty—the family reunited. Every week or so I visited Agnes and her father. My writing consumed my days and many evenings, too, and Tommy and Sophy regularly invited me for dinner.

On Christmas Day my aunt popped her head in as I was finishing an edit of my latest story. "Going to Canterbury on this glorious winter's day, Trot?" she asked.

"Yes, great weather for a Trot to have a gallop!" I laughed.

She smiled and turned away.

"Uh, Aunt—" I began as she stepped toward the kitchen. She came back, eyebrows raised. "Do you know anything more about that special person of Agnes'? The one you mentioned a while ago."

There was a pause and some sort of a look of resolve settled on my aunt's face. She crossed the room to my desk and looked at me squarely.

"I think I do," she said. "At least I'm certain there is one. And I wouldn't be surprised if there was a wedding in the offing."

That news was a shock.

"She never talks about him and after all we've confided to one another for so many years, I think it's awfully strange." I knew I sounded whiny.

"Have you thought of asking her?" was my aunt's parting question.

The ride was icy and stirring. The horse needed little guidance over the road and so my thoughts were free to arrive ahead of me. I *was* going to ask why she didn't trust me enough to tell me about this love of hers. If she thought I was still too deep in mourning for Dora to be glad for her joy, then she didn't know how much I wanted her to be happy. I would tell her I felt shut out from her life by this secret. I may have lost the chance to love her as I wished but I couldn't bear to lose the gift of her friendship, too.

I found her lighting candles on the tree in the entry hall, and we shared a holiday kiss.

"Agnes, leave that for now and come sit with me, please," I said as I led her into the drawing-room. She searched my face when we sat down.

"You have a secret, Agnes," I said. "Let me share it."

She looked down and I felt her tremble.

"I know there's someone you're in love with and I want to be in on your happiness over it. Please, Agnes, don't close me out."

"There's no one," she said, adding in a very soft voice, "at least there's no happiness in it."

She pulled her hand from mine and walked to the glass garden doors. Her shoulders shook and she put her hands to her face.

"Please, Trot. My secret is nothing new," she said between sniffles. "Through the years it's always been the same. Let this be as it is."

"Agnes, have I hurt you when I only want to be happy for you and with you?"

I knew she would run from the room unless I stopped her, so I put one arm around her waist. She looked at me and I heard the echo of her words *through the years...always the same*. New thoughts and hopes went spinning in my mind.

"Agnes, I never thought I would say this to you—at least not before we were too old to be glad of it." Her eyes were wide and bright. "Every time I've ridden out of Canterbury, I've gone away loving you. And every time I've come back in, I've come back loving you. There has been only you for so very many years."

"Trot," she said, "I've loved you all my life."

I've told this story looking back. I still see my Aunt Betsey's face lit with a million sparks of joy when Agnes and I went to Dover that Christmas night. And Peggotty's "whoops" and giggles. And Mr. Bick's grin so large not a molar was hidden. I see the Canterbury chapel full of roses and orchids, and hear the wedding vows. Traddles' toast to our long and loving lives rings like church bells in my ears.

The years are passing. Agnes and I are grey-haired now, but she is still a beauty. Our children are the favorite boys and girls of Peggotty and Aunt Betsey. My pen writes on, sometimes it seems to propel itself. And all my days and all my nights are peaceful, since love and Agnes turned up.